Also by Joan Byrd
From Indigo Sea Press

The All My Tomorrows Series:

A New Beginning

Love Finds a Way

Lost Stories of Jesus

The Box in the Attic

The Good Seed—the Bad Seed

indigoseapress.com

Today, Tomorrow and Always

By

Joan Byrd

Deep Indigo Books
Published by Indigo Sea Press
Winston-Salem

Deep Indigo Books
Indigo Sea Press
PO Box 26701
Winston-Salem, NC 27114

First Deep Indigo Books edition published December, 2019
Deep Indigo Books, Moon Sailor and all production design are trademarks of Indigo Sea Press, used under license.

For information regarding bulk purchases of this book, digital purchase and special discounts, please contact the publisher at indigoseapress@gmail.com

Cover design by Pan Morelli
Manufactured in the United States of America
ISBN 978-1-63066-496-1

Chapter One

TarSa, 1975

Reverend Gene Scott drove his new 1975 Chevy down Palm Tree Road. Unlike two years ago, the sun was shining and Gene was no longer a lonely widower. His love for Susan grew with each passing day, no two were the same. They still cherished their time together, either making passionate love in their private bedroom or just holding hands going for a stroll down the sidewalk in front of their white farmhouse.

Now at thirty-eight and Susan at nineteen, he still wondered how lucky he was to have found her. He knew the first time they looked at one another there was something special between them. They both had felt it, although Susan had known from the beginning it was love. Even though he tried to convince himself otherwise, due to their age difference. Gene finally came to reality and admitted his love to Susan and the fact he wanted her to be a part of his life forever.

Lost in his thoughts, Gene did not notice the car sitting on the side road until it speeded out in front of him, causing him to slam on his brakes. Instantly his eyes went up to the rear-view mirror and was glad another car wasn't driving behind him. Gritting his teeth, Scott slapped the steering wheel.

"That damn Weber! This meeting had better be about a conference or something related to church!"

The Sand Palms Methodist Church had grown to two-thousand members since Reverend Gene Scott began preaching there along with his good friend, Reverend John Crain. John and Edna Crain, along with their son David, were Gene and Susan's allies, along with Pogo Goings, Scott's pal and best friend, when they were trying to figure out their life together.

After building Sand Palms Church to sit well over two thousand members, the leaders over the Methodist church on

1

the main land, received this small island church into the United Methodist, and due to their performance, Scott and Crain would be able to stay there for the unforeseeable future.

Scott pulled his Chevy up in front of the Weber's new large mansion in TarSa.

"This little visit better not be another mission trip and take me away from Susan." He mumbled as he climbed his six-foot-seven frame out the car door. Gene noticed the new red sports car parked inside an open garage and a similar one parked right behind it.

"Looks like little Miss Weber has a new boyfriend. That may make this trip over worth it." Gene chuckled as he made his way up to the massive oak door. "Maybe the little red-head can keep her hands off me for a while."

Gene's thoughts turned to Susan as he smiled, remembering how jealous and mad she became every time Gloria touched him. "My little gal, always ready to claim her man. That's my girl!" he laughed softly as he rang the doorbell and waited. "Shit, where the devil is Johnson? I just called over here and said I was on my way!" he rang it again and the door slung open. Gloria Ann Weber threw her arms around Gene's neck.

"There you are, my favorite preacher!" she giggled "How nice of you to come for a visit, darling."

"I am here because it was an order from the bishop!" Gene Scott pushed passed the flirty red-head and looked around the large entrance hall "Where the devil is your father, Gloria? I don't have all day!"

Looking around, Gene noticed a silent young man dressed for tennis. It was obvious he had witnessed the scene between his date and this handsome, angry man from his unfriendly demeaner.

"Sorry fellow, I didn't see you standing in the corner." Gene chuckled at the man's sour expression as he put out his hand for a handshake. "Scott, Gene Scott."

2

"Yes, I know who you are." He stared down at Scott's hand and backed away, refusing to shake hands.

Pulling his hand down, Gene smiled broadly "You must be Gloria's latest boyfriend." He looked around at the redhead standing behind him "Aren't you going to introduce me to your friend?"

"Yes, Gene darling." Gloria moved up close to the handsome preacher and placed her soft hand on his arm. Smiling up with her seductive green eyes, she said softly "Where are my manners?"

"Didn't know you had any!" Gene chuckled and brushed her hand away as he looked down at the red-face stranger "Look fellow, you have nothing to worry about as far as I'm concern. I am a happily married man with two kids."

"Oh? That's good!" the young man blushed "I mean, Gloria seem so familiar with you, I thought…"

"Yes, I know what you thought." Gene walked over to the stairs and stared up for any sign of the bishop as he continued "My little Susan is all the woman this old man needs." His hand slapped the handrail loudly "Weber, get your slow ass down here or I am going home!"

Henry Weber peeked from his bedroom door. "Reverend Scott, I'm really quite sorry for my delay." He forced a laugh "My little Gloria wanted to see you first."

"Bishop Weber, stop wasting my time!" Gene grew impatient with the robust bishop "I have got a sexy wife waiting for me at home and more to do than standing around here watching you eat candy!"

Henry Weber grunted as he laid the box of chocolates on the hall table and walked quickly down the steps. His face was flushed with embarrassment over Scott's language in front of company.

"Scott, do you really have to say things like that in front of Gloria's friend?"

"Gloria's friend! Which brings me to another unanswered

question! What the shit is his name, or is it some big secret? And what did you summons me for this time, sir?" Gene was getting angry from all the run around.

"This young man is Phillip Sanders a tennis pro from a wealthy, respectable family." Henry Weber patted Sanders' shoulder "I am sure you both have a lot in common, Scott."

"In common? Just from your description of young Phillip, I would all but guarantee we have absolutely nothing in common!" Gene Scott smiled at the shaken up young man "Nothing personal towards you, sonny boy, it just the fact you think Gloria is wonderful and I do not!"

"Daddy, are you going to let Gene talk like that about me?" Gloria Ann pouted.

"Look, Bishop Weber, enough of this nonsense!" Scott gritted his teeth "Are you going to spit out why you sent for me or do I walk out that door?"

"Alright Scott! Gloria, take Phillip out for a tennis game or drinks by the pool." The bishop looked pleadingly at his stubborn daughter "O.K. sweetheart, will you do that for daddy?"

"Just take your leave now Gloria before I escort you out myself!" Gene's eyes burned down on the spoiled redhead.

"Alright, I'm going." Gloria backed away from Gene's angry stare "We know when we're not wanted!" she turned up her head in defiance and pulled the tennis pro out the side door. Weber watched his daughter closely as he closed the door.

"I think we have hurt her feelings."

"Weber, you jackass!" Scott headed for the front door as Henry Weber chased after him and grabbed his strong arm to stop him. Gene narrowed his eyes on him "What's it going to be bishop, the reason you ask me here or more sympathy for you spoiled daughter?"

"Alright Scott, come back and I'll tell you why I called you."

Gene looked down at the man who had given him a giant

4

size headache "Go ahead, I'm waiting, Bishop Weber."

"It is a new mission Scott." Before the bishop could say another word, Gene Scott took him by the collar.

"Listen sir, I told you I was finished doing mission work!" Scott frowned down at the heavy bishop "I am a married man now with a family and I be damned if I am going away on some dangerous mission! Do you hear what I saying Weber? No! Damn it!"

"Scott, if it were up to me…" he swallowed nervously "I would never ask you, but, it is our leaders Scott, the entire conference want you and only you for this mission!"

"Why me?" he spoke loudly "There are plenty of men wanting to go! Martin, for instance!"

"George Martin? Scott, for heaven's sake." The bishop laughed nervously "You are the man for the job. The votes were unanimous! Your past missions were a flying success! The F.B.I. have requested you! Scott, for the love of God, do your chosen mission!"

"Building me up Henry? How touching!" Scott turned to leave "Forget it! My family is my life now and if the church has a problem with that, I will quit!"

"Scott, you can never quit!" Weber took a firm grip of his arm and looked up with sincerity "If it means that much to you Scott, to be with your family, safe and sound, I…" the bishop reached for an open box of chocolate cremes and put one in his mouth "Mumm, tasty. Like I was saying…I'm sorry, would you care for a soft chocolate?" Weber held out the box and the irritated minister pushed the box away.

"No thank you sir! Just say what you were about to tell me."

"You are too valuable to the church to lose Scott. You build up every church you walk into." Henry Weber shook his head as he tried to understand why people were so excited with this man. "Everyone just seems to love you and you are always getting things accomplished." The bishop could tell Gene

5

Scott was growing impatient with his long drawn out praise, so he thought best to leave well enough alone and say something Scott was waiting to hear.

"Reverend Scott, I will inform the church that you chose to remain here with your family."

Gene relaxed and smiled down at the bishop. "Well, Bishop Weber, I guess you can be thoughtful, when push comes to shove."

"It looks like God will have to find someone else to fight for him, to do His work, go to bat for Him." The bishop turned his head away and smiled to himself as he continued "Isn't that what you're always preaching Scott? To be part of the team! Get off the side lines, don't expect God to do it for us?"

"Weber, you Jackass. Use my words to make me look like a hypocrite!" Gene Scott gritted his teeth "If I decide to take this mission, Susan comes with me!"

"Like hell she does!" Weber's voice grew loud "Trust me Scott, the place that you will be going is not fit for a lady!"

"I go, she goes!" Scott spit out "She stays, I stay!"

"Scott, you are a strong headed man! Can't you stay out of your wife's panties for a few weeks?" Henry Weber suddenly regretted his remark when Gene Scott lifted him off the floor, his free fist staying just inches away from the bishop's nose.

"Look Weber, my reason for wanting my wife by my side is something you could never understand! It's not all sex between us, there's so much more! When I say Susan is my life, I mean it! We had to give up a lot of our first year together for you, Weber. I love my kids; they are a part of me and Susan and I love my little woman more than anyone or anything on this earth! She is second in my heart only to my Lord!"

"Yes, I know how close you are to Susan and I'm sorry I chose the wrong words, Scott!" Gene sat him down and the bishop brushed himself off "I know your love for her is great, but you said it yourself Scott, you love the Lord more! I think once you know what the mission is, you will understand why you shouldn't take your young wife. It's not that dangerous, it's just the circumstances."

"Fine! Even if I can talk her into staying at home, I will tell her everything about the mission." Gene checked his watch. He had promised Susan he would try to be home within an hour. "I keep no secrets from my wife, sir, it makes for a bad relationship. There's got to be trust."

"Of course, you are right Scott, in most circumstances I would agree 100%.' The bishop could tell Scott was getting anxious to leave "I know you must be in a hurry to get home to your lovely wife so I will fill you in on all the details later. You will have help on this mission from two of your close friends, Sorensen and Tabor. They have been chosen to go with you, without their wives, of course."

"Good luck with that one." Scott chuckled and opened the front door. Stepping out into the fresh air, he took a deep breath. "We will talk later then, Bishop Weber. I am off to get into my wife's panties!" Scott smiled broadly down at Weber's blushing face and walked to his car whistling, got in and drove away.

Chapter Two

Gene Scott pulled his Chevy to a stop in front of his and Susan's white farmhouse. A little beagle came running across the yard barking.

"Shags, boy!" Gene squatted down to pat the dog's small head "Out on a hunt buddy?" he looked up and smiled when Susan came running from the front door.

"Gene, you are home!" she threw her arms around his strong chest "You are right on time, exactly one hour!"

"My sweet Susan has been watching the clock?" he picked her up and kissed her tenderly "I've been gone just one hour and you already miss your old man."

"Damn right, husband!" Susan laughed at Gene's frown "Shocked at my language, Reverend? The preacher I married talks that way 'all' the time, and he is supposed to be setting perfect examples for me to follow!"

"I'll perfect example your sweet butt!" Gene slapped her playfully on the back side "What are your plans today beautiful and where are our kids?"

"The twins are sleeping upstairs and the only plans I have today is to be with my sexy, wonderful husband!" Susan slapped Gene on his back side.

"Sexy huh?" he laughed "Well, like I was telling Bishop Weber, I had to get home and get into my wife's panties."

"Gene Scott, you did no such thing!" Susan recognized her husband's sneaky grin "Gene Scott, you did!" She slapped his arm "The bishop, what the hel…, what the shi…" she swallowed "Well, what did that man call you over for?"

"The usual." Scott tried to sound casual "Just another mission job."

"Gene Scott, I hope you told that fat, candy eating bishop where to go!" Susan stomped her foot "He knows that you are married now and got a family! Why that jerk! The very ideal, a stupid mission!"

"Susan darling, relax. I did tell him no." Gene watched his wife relax.

"Thank God." Susan smiled "I knew I could depend on my sweet, loving, supporting, never want to leave my side, husband."

"I did tell him no, and I must admit, I was not on my best behavior." Gene watched her closely, as she giggled.

"I know you can say a few choice words when someone pushes your buttons."

"Exactly." Gene pulled her into his arms so he would not have to look into her eyes for what he was about to tell her "And it was going my way until that damn Weber threw my sermons back in my face."

Susan pulled out of his arms and stared up at him "Gene, you didn't! You couldn't! Tell me now, are you going to take this mission?"

Gene laughed softly and Susan hit his arm.

"Susan, sweetheart, the Methodist leaders voted for me, it was unanimous. I cannot let God down Susan." He grew serious.

"Then I am going with you! That is final Gene Scott!" Susan watched him carefully "I will follow you if you do not take me with you, and you know I mean it!"

"Yes, I know my head strong little Susan." Gene took her hands and she tried to pull free, but he held her tight. "I know how much you love your old man Susan, because I love you the exact same way! The bishop says this is not that dangerous, but it's no place for a lady."

"Who said I was a lady?" tears filled Susan's eyes.

"I do Susan! I say you are lady, my lady!" Gene gazed at her seriously "Shit, sweetheart, I never want you out of my sight, you know that!"

"Do I?" tears started rolling down her cheeks.

"Susan, my Susan, God, I love you so much! I never knew

love could be this beautiful. I was alive for thirty-six years before I knew what true love was." Gene took around her and hugged her tightly "It was love a first sight, Susan! I didn't know it then but I know it now! I just want everything perfect for you!"

"You are what's perfect for me Gene! You!" Susan returned his warm embrace "What...what is the mission?"

"I don't know yet darling, believe me." Gene kissed the top of Susan's head "I promise, as soon as I find out, you will be the first to know."

"You promise?" she looked up into his love filled eyes "You're not just trying to butter me up, you really mean it Gene? You will tell me the truth."

"I promise you Susan Scott." Gene bent over and kissed her passionately "Oh my sweet Susan, listen, let me go and find out what the mission is about and then I will send for you if at all possible."

"I guess that will have to do for now." Susan laid her head over on Gene's strong shoulder "You do want me to come, don't you Gene?"

"Susan, darling, you know how much, but for now we've got to wait on Henry Weber."

"Weber! I'm beginning to hate that name!" Susan took his hand and pulled her husband toward the house "Why don't he get a job working in a candy factory?"

Gene Scott chuckled as he pictured the robust bishop sampling candy as it raced passed him on a conveying machine.

"Yeh, good old Weber could be the chief candy taster. Who knows, they may hire Gloria while they're at it. She thinks she is so sweet, maybe they'll make a candy after her."

"Could we be so lucky?" Susan looked up into her husband's blue eyes "Alright, let's go inside so my sexy husband can get into my panties!"

Holding tight to each other, Gene and Susan laughed as they walked through their front door.

Chapter Three

The Sand Palms United Methodist Church was filled with worshippers on this bright May morning. Everyone loved coming to church now that Reverend Gene Scott had started services with his long- time friend, John Crain. Crain smiled at the full congregation and patted his friend's strong arm.

"Gene, you really know how to bring the lost sheep home."

"Give them a little bible and grain, showing them the direction they need to go and they will follow." Gene smiled brightly as his eyes searched the crowded room and fell lovingly on Susan. Their eyes locked in passion as he thought to himself "It only grows more and more. Damn, I love that woman!" he snapped out of his thoughts when he felt his friend nudge his arm lightly.

"Ready Gene? The choir is finished."

"You bet buddy, hit it!" Scott laughed softly as John Crain cleared his throat and stood up.

"My dear friends, today is both bittersweet and rewarding." Confused by his words, the people look at each other for a possible explanation. "I know how much you have grown to love Reverend Scott. We all love and admire this big guy." John smiled down at Gene "God has called brother Scott to take on another missionary journey."

There were moans throughout the large congregation.

"I know we shall miss him gravely while he is away, righting the wrong that Satan has cast before him, but he has been chosen as the best man to take on this fight. We all know Reverend Scott enjoys a good fight when he is in the ring with God. Let us all pray for a speedy victory and his safe return to us and his loving wife, Susan and their adorable twins." Reverend Crain turned to his dear friend, tears in his eyes as he announced to the silent crowd "Without future words, I will turn it over to Reverend Scott."

There came a loud burst of applause from the congregation when Gene stood up at the pulpit. He smiled out at the many faces and held up his hands for silence.

"Boy, I feel like a rock star!" Gene's response brought laughter from the crowd but only briefly. The sad reality that their beloved minister would be apart from them made them depressed. "Wow, this is a sad bunch of faces. Is this the way you want to send me off to fight the good fight and remember this sad lot?" he slapped the pulpit "Friends, lighten up, put a smile on those beautiful Christian faces! I have been called to lead God's team on this mission and we will win, by God! Remember friends, we cannot sit back and cheer on God! We need to get out there and fight, for God, for Him! Let God do the cheering! Remember what I've told you many times, we are His hands! His voice! We are soldiers of the cross! So, take up your cross and follow Him! Make Him proud! Be a player and be proud to be a Christian! Live for God and He will give you the victory!" Gene's smile was contagious "Well, I see a few smiling faces out there. Hey, watch those tears! You don't want to get this big guy crying." Gene reached for the hymnal "Turn to page 222, another one of my favorites, My Hope Is Built."

The organist began to play and the congregation tried to sing as they choked back their tears, only Gene Scott's voice rang out strong. He held up his hand to stop the music and looked out.

"Friends, I do not think the Lord can hear that pitiful singing. Let's sing the last verse and this time, show me what happy Christians are supposed to sound like. At least if you are all singing out, it might be equal to my big mouth!"

Everyone started laughing at the thought of two thousand voices being equal to one strong voice and as requested, the last verse was song with more joy.

"That's more like it! Now I can go into battle with Lucifer

knowing I have your prayers and blessings, filled with that beautiful sound ringing in my ears." Reverend Scott grew serious as his attention fell on his wife "Dear friends, as I said, remember to pray for me and my partners, for our mission and I promise, I will return to this pulpit as soon as possible." Gene's gaze had not left Susan's beautiful face as he spoke "I am asking everyone to pray for my family and help watch over them while I am away. Susan is my life, my children are my life," his attention fell back on the church members "and you are my church family, and I love each and every one." He raised his hands for the benediction.

"Now, go in peace and may God guide you throughout this day and always! In Jesus most Holy name, Amen!"

Gene met Susan and the twins in front of the church as the members were departing. He held tight to her hand as each member passed by to speak and tried to put on a cheerful face. Susan's parents stopped to speak and Shirley patted her son-in-law's hand.

"Don't you worry about your family Gene, darling. We will take good care of our Susan and the children while you are away fighting the bad guys."

"Indeed we will!" Owen shook Scott's hand "It will be like old times looking after our little girl."

"Dad, I really don't need looking after." Susan squeezed Gene's hand "I can take care of Samson and Delilah just fine." She smiled over at Pogo, talking to a girl "Besides, I have Pogo, he's a big help."

"Yes Shirley, Owen, my little Susan can handle about anything she sets her mind on." Gene chuckled "If she can handle her old man, she can handle anything."

"Gene, you are not an old man!" Susan frowned up at him "You are plenty young enough for me!"

"Listen to her Gene, having a wife as young as Susan will keep you young." Owen winked at the tall handsome man "Yes, young and active!"

13

"Owen?" Shirley blushed, then turned back to her daughter "Susan dear, I am sure Polard is good at cooking and perhaps even yard work and helping you clean the house, but my dear, there is Sam and Di, who are at the age to wonder off in the woods surrounding your farm or get out in the road!"

"Mother, why do you insist on calling Samson and Delilah, Sam and Di?" Susan frowned "You know perfectly well what we named them!"

"Yes dear, you did tell me." Shirley reached down and patted the twins on their head "Because you called Gene your Samson and he called you his Delilah, which is fine for a man and woman, but my dear, they are just babies, brother and sister. It just sounds so odd."

"Odd or not mom, that is their names." Susan noticed her brother running over from talking to a group of boys his age.

"Hi sis, hi Reverend Scott!" Jobi shook his big friend's hand. "Another great sermon sir, short and to the point! Wow, going on another mission! Need some help?"

"Young man, I think you've had enough mission work behind your parent's back to last a lifetime." Owen looked into Gene's serious eyes, knowing his very sermon was on doing God's work. "Maybe when you are older and much wiser, like Scott here."

"Your dad's right little buddy. Maybe when you grow up into fighting shoes!" Scott took a hold on Jobi's shoulder "Say, how would you like to come home with us and spend the night with your old pal Scott?"

"Gosh! Heavy!" he looked up pleadingly at his parents "Can I, please?" his young eyes begged "I promise to behave! Honest mom, dad!" Jobi smiled over at his sister "I'll even sleep with my pal Pogo so Susan and Gene can have one last romantic night together."

"Alright little brother, you have said enough!" Susan playfully hit the top of his head lightly "You might be fourteen now Jobi, but you do not have to go into personal details. I think mom and dad get the point without you spelling it for them!"

As the last- minute stragglers filed out of the church to speak to Scott, two young teenage girls stood whispering on the opposite steps from the Scott family. They had their eyes on the handsome preacher.

"That Reverend Scott is about the sexiest man I've ever seen!" one of the girls lend over close to her smiling friend who was nodding a positive. "Susan is the luckiest girl alive, on any planet!"In a dream like state the other teen responded.

"The luckiest, for sure, and she is not much older than we are. I wish I were Mrs. Gene Scott."

Gene had noticed the young girls observing him closely, heads together as they whispered. He had even heard the last girl's remark about being Mrs. Gene Scott, so he knew what to do to break their trance.

"Did you girls say something?" Gene smiled over at the shy girls who blushed from getting caught by the handsome preacher. They grab each other's hand and raced off. Susan had looked to see who her husband was talking to and noticed the look of embarrassment on the two seventeen- year- old girls before they sped off to the parking lot.

"What was that all about Gene?" Susan whisper up to him.

"No big deal, I just seem to attract the young ladies." Gene knew Susan would get jealous over their flirting.

"Oh really?" Susan eyes narrowed, first at the girls for staring back at her man and the big stupid grin on Scott's face. "So, you think it's funny, mister? I suppose you are already looking for a younger model! Perhaps, one without kids hanging on to her apron strings!"

Gene Scott was glad the people had finished with their greetings so he could tease his wife.

"Relax pretty woman, I think I have got all the young woman I can handle and she's defiantly the model I want to keep!" Gene wanted to kiss Susan, right then and there, but he

15

was in the Church yard and his in-laws were just a few feet away talking to their son about staying over at the Scott's.

"If it will be no problem and you are sure it will be alright…" Shirley smiled down at the happy young man "Jobi may stay over at your house tonight."

"Mom, it will be fine.' Susan hugged her brother "We always love having Jobi over."

"Very well, we will bring Jobi over right after we have lunch and get his overnight bag." Owen kissed his daughter and grandchildren as they were saying goodbye. Pogo came running up, smiling from ear to ear.

Scott hit his friend's arm playfully "Pogo, what the devil are you smiling so big about?"

"Sweetheart, didn't you see him talking to Allison Rollins?" Susan tease the young man, causing his face to blush "They were standing 'real' close."

"Real close? Really?" Gene grinned broadly at his blushing friend "Got yourself a date with that cute little blonde, buddy?"

"Not exactly." Pogo smiled proudly "I'm working on my strategy. She asked me what I was doing Saturday night and I played it real cool. I told her I had to check my calendar, you know, as though I might be busy!"

"Pogo, you idiot! Call that playing cool?" Gene frowned down at him and shook his head in dismay as he picked up Samson and started walking toward their big station wagon. Pogo ran behind him, trying to catch up "Look pal, boys never use that line dummy, girls do!"

"But, I thought…" Gene cut Pogo off before he could finish his statement.

"That's your problem Pogo, you don't think! You just jump in with both feet and say really stupid things!" Gene snapped as Susan stood listening to her outspoken husband.

After fasting the children in the car seats, Gene relaxed and put his strong arm around Pogo's drooping shoulders.

"Look pal, it's too late to make things right here, Allison has already left with her parents. Now you need a strategy that works, so listen to a pro. Wait until tonight, then call her and tell her you want to take her out for a burger and a movie Saturday night!" Gene winked at his friend "A piece of cake!"

"No Pogo, absolutely not! Gene is way off!" Susan frowned up at her husband who looked back at her helpless. She gently took Pogo's arm "Now listen to me Pogo, I am a girl and I know how to win Allison's heart. Call her up as soon as we get home, tell her you are taking her to Rhythms Saturday night to have a romantic dinner and dancing afterward." She smiled up at her husband who stood silently, listening to her advice. "Now Pogo, when you dance with Allison, make sure it's a slow dance and let her talk about things she likes. Try to act interested in what she is saying, then when you take her home and she allows you to kiss her, make it once, for goodnight." Susan patted Pogo's shoulder "Trust me Pogo, Allison will fall for you and there will be other dates with the pretty blonde."

"Boy, I really blew it!" Gene stared at Susan after hearing her plan "How did I ever get you to fall for a cheap guy like me?"

"For starters Gene Scott, you were not exactly cheap, but the way I felt about you..." Susan reached up to caress his handsome face "I would have gone to a dog fight with you and had Cracker-Jacks for supper, if you ask me."

"That love at first sight thing saved my butt!" Gene grabbed his laughing wife and twirled her around as Pogo watched smiling, and climbed into the back seat, next to the twins.

Gene helped Susan in the car then climbed inside "Let's go home and roast some hot dogs, I'm starved!" he pulled out of the parking lot and drove home.

17

Chapter Four

Gene Scott opened his eyes slowly and looked over at the bedside clock, 5:00 a.m. He turned over quietly and looked at Susan, sleeping soundly beside him. Smiling to himself, he remembered them falling asleep in each other's arms after making love. As his eyes feasted on her beauty, he thought

"My beautiful Susan, how did I get so lucky to get your love? How can I leave your side again, ever, if only for a short time?" his eyes fell on her young breast, uncovered, warm, firm and round. He reached over and touched the one closes to him, causing Susan to move a little from his touch. Gene smiled at the other breast "Feeling left out, are you?" he whispered as he propped up so his other hand could reach over and claim it. "Now, my little nipples, come to papa." Gene lend over and let his tongue caress her nipple.

Susan's body moved and Gene looked up to find her smiling in her sleep. She whispered softly, "Gene, Gene."

He smiled broadly then turned his attention back on the harden nipple, his hand wrapped around the other breast. Susan lazily opened her eyes and looked down at her husband's head over her right breast. She smiled as she ran her fingers through his curls hanging down on his neck and whispered

"Sweetheart, the other little nipple is feeling left out."

Gene looked up into her eyes and smiled, his own eyes speaking the love he was feeling that swelled in his heart and his manly need for her.

"I must not let any part of my sexy Delila feel neglected." He moved his lips to her other breast.

Susan's heart was beating with desire as her fingers ran wildly through Gene's messy hair.

"I think I need my husband, my sexy Samson to move over

to the rest of Delila!" she pulled his head up, then wiggled out from under him "Like now Gene! Roll over mister!"

Gene rolled over on his back, laughing "Never stand in a 'hot' mama's way!" Susan stretched out over him. Gene pulled her as close as he could, his breathing heavy with passion. "Susan, you are one hell of a woman!" pulling her head down, he parted his lips over hers in a fiery kiss. "And you are 'all' mine!"

"Every inch, Reverend Scott!" Susan moved her body over him slowly and she could feel her husband was more than ready to make love "And you are one hell of a man!" she bit his ear softly "And you are all mine, every beautiful inch!"

Gene laughed lazily as he slid himself inside her "God Susan, you feel so good."

They moved in perfect rhythm as they filled one another with perfect love. One more act of showing their deep compassion and desire before Gene had to leave her again.

Susan rolled off and kissed her husband as tears filled her blue eyes "Oh Gene, this will be the last time until you come back home to me." She propped up on her elbow, looking hopeful "Maybe you will call me to say I can come and join you."

"Susan, it won't be easy for me either, darling." Gene ran his fingers through his hair "That damn Weber, always a thorn in my side and a pain in my ass!" he sat up on the side of the bed.

"I wish the entire Weber family would swim back to California!" Susan stacked up the pillows behind her as she watched her naked husband moved toward the bathroom "they cannot let us be happy!"

Gene called out from the bathroom as he turned on the shower "Well, maybe I'll kick his sorry butt across the Pacific!" he teased "I will keep my eyes open for that candy factory looking for a chief candy taster! He will jump right on it and probably eat up all the profits!" he laughed as he climbed inside the shower "Shit! Cold water!"

Susan laughed and fell back on the pillows.

The day flew by as Gene Scott packed and got ready for his mission trip. He knew he would be meeting Michael and James at the airport, so he had arranged for Henry Weber to pick him up on his way. Gene didn't want Susan or Pogo to see who his partners were and let it slip to Jackie and Ali, knowing their women would start searching for their men and track them down. Scott pulled Pogo to one side when Susan was busy with the kid's bath.

"Now listen Pogo, I am depending on you buddy to look after Susan and the kids while I'm away."

"Scott, let me come with you!" Pogo put his arm around the big guy's shoulder "We're good working together, remember?"

"You were a great partner Pogo, when we rescued those virgins and Martin." Scott laughed when he pictured himself and Pogo sitting in that sleazy bar drinking beer and looking like a couple of drug-taking creeps. "And you were great as Larry when we were after those drug pins! But pal, not this time. Henry Weber has got me plenty of help. I really need you to stay here for my girl."

Pogo read Scott's serious eyes so he relented and excepted the task before him.

"You can rely on me Scott. Susan is in good hands."

"I know buddy, that's why I want you here to watch after them." Scott rubbed his fingers through Pogo's hair. "I trust you with my girl. You know I will beat the shit out of you if you so much as look at her in the wrong way."

"That will never happen, man!" Pogo laughed "I want to live out the rest of my days, besides, there's Allison, remember?"

"Oh yes, Allison!" Gene's eyes lit up in mischief "How did your date go? Was my girl right or your old pal here?"

"Susan's ideal worked like a charm, man! Scott, you are a lady's man by fate, looks, personally or something hidden." Pogo smiled "Your Susan's advice made my date absolutely perfect!"

"Well, try and control your feelings for cute Allison. Don't let them get in the way of your main job,

Watching my family while I'm away."

"Don't sweat it Scott, Allison understands I have responsibilities."

"Hey you two, what are my favorite fellows up to?" Susan walked up a looped her arms around her husband.

"Scott is giving me last minute orders. I was just about to offer my services as his taxi driver to the airport."

"I will take him Pogo." Susan smiled up at Gene "I need to be there with you until the last moment."

"Listen to you both!" Gene laughed "You act as though I am leaving forever." His eyes fell on Susan, her eyes filling up with tears and he knew he must fight his own tears from coming. "Hey beautiful, no tears. I will have to rush to the plane as soon as I arrive at the airport. There won't be time for long goodbyes honey so Henry Weber is coming by to take me."

"Gene, sweetheart, why?" Susan could not control her tears "Why Weber? Why not me?"

"Because I need to tell you goodbye here, Susan. Here, where I can hold you and kiss you. Here where I can rush back to and find you waiting for me, where I left you." No matter how hard Gene Scott had tried, he could not control his own tears "Come back to our home, Susan darling!" he held her tight in his arms as Pogo listened to their sad fair well and growing misty eyed, he spoke up.

"Sometimes I feel like killing Henry Weber! He's always sticking his candy covered nose in your life, Scott!"

Gene laughed out, trying to picture the bishop with chocolate on his big nose. He patted his upset friend's back.

21

Pogo, pal, give it a rest, my constant friend. You can help me by praying that George Martin won't be there to help me!"

"Gene Scott!" Susan laughed, along with Pogo, at the very thought of Martin working on this mission with Gene. "Maybe they can spare Doctor Danfield to help you."

"Then call me the Lone Ranger!" Scott put his arm around both of them and gave them a big hug. He pulled away to lift his son out of the red wagon. "Shit, the little fellow looks just like his old man!" he chuckled when the toddler giggled "Samson, my boy, my handsome little Scott!" he kissed the boy's chubby cheek "Now son, daddy wants you to watch after mama and Pogo for me! They could use watching!" Gene laughed and handed his son to Pogo, then reached down for his daughter, who looked just like Susan.

"There is my pretty little Susan, my Delilah!" he lifted her up and kissed her rosy cheek "Watch out for older men!"

Susan laughed as he handed her the small child. She sat Delilah back in the red wagon and took Gene's strong arm.

"Sweetheart, do you know what this mission is about yet?"

"Not yet little darling. The dear bishop is keeping me in the dark, big secret!" Gene looked into her alluring blue eyes "As soon as I find out, I promise to call you." He pulled her into a tight embrace, the thoughts of leaving her tearing at his heart. "Once I begin this job, I might not be able to call, but I will let you know sweetheart." Gene kissed her tenderly and heard a car coming up the driveway. Gene checked his watch. Bishop Weber was right on time.

"Oh shit, Weber just pulled into the driveway. Damn, our time flew!" Gene kissed Susan again and hugged her lovingly as he whispered in her ear "Just remember last night and this morning. It will keep us close until I come back to you darling."

"I will hold those moments in my heart sweetheart and wait to hear from you." Susan kept her arms tight around his strong chest, not wanting to let go. "Gene, I love you!"

"I love you Susan!" he kissed her as Henry Weber cleared his throat.

"Scott, we are going to miss that airplane if you do not stop necking now!"

"Hold on to your damn pants, Bishop Weber!" Gene picked up his suitcase, then kissed his wife one last time before moving toward the bishop "Now get that big butt into this car and start driving!" Reverend Scott climbed in the car and waved at a weeping Susan, through tears of his own.

Chapter Five

Reverend Gene Scott climbed quickly on the airplane with Henry Weber trailing behind him. His big smile was genuine when he greeted his close friends, Michael Sorensen and James Tabor. Looking around the private plane, he noticed they were the only ones on board besides the pilot in the cockpit.

"Well now, I see you guys can get away from those beautiful wives of yours!"

Michael and James smiled at one another as Michael spoke up.

"My lovely wife Jackie, yes." He picked up a magazine and looked from the small window "I still can't understand why I couldn't take my plane. I feel out of place as a passenger."

Weber had been listening as he boarded the small plane and watched the pilot shut and secure the plane's door. Taking a seat, he looked up at Michael.

"Sorensen, those wives of yours will track you down if we take your plane and follow us. We cannot have any of our women involved in this case." Weber shook his head and pulled out a candy bar from his bulging coat pocket. "Take your plane, seriously? I cannot believe you haven't figured this one out! You are supposed to be hot shot detectives! Your I.D. number is on your plane! They can easily be tracked down and those ladies are pretty clever when it comes to missing husbands!"

"We get it Weber! You do not have to draw us a picture!" James rolled his eyes at Gene Scott, who was observing the bishop's raging. James watched the overbearing bishop pull out another candy bar after dropping his empty wrapper on the floor. "If you must know sir, Jackie and Ali think we're still on the island, working on a building team. They won't be searching for us."

"Can't be too careful." Tossing down the second wrapper, Henry Weber opened another candy bar as Scott moved around in his seat, growing impatient for answers.

"Bishop Weber! For God's sake, stop feeding your face!" Gene's voice was powerful, causing the heavy bishop to jump "Just tell us what this mission is about! Make it simple, no dramatics! Got it?"

"Boy, where is your patience, Scott?" Henry Weber wiped the chocolate off his face "We have got a few hours in the air. There is no need to dive right into the details!"

"Weber, you ask me where my patience was! I lost my damn patience the moment you stepped on this plane and opened your big mouth!" Gene Scott gritted his teeth "Now start talking before I kick your ass off this plane! No more secrets, Bishop Weber! We are waiting!"

"Alright Scott, just calm down before you make the pilot nervous. I will tell you everything I know." Weber straightened his short frame to appear taller when he stood. "This is like a double mission. There are drugs involved and…a…prostitutes, lot of prostitutes." He could feel the tension building among the three men listening as Gene Scott spoke out, eyes a flame.

"What kind of mission is this for three married men, Weber? We would never fool around with these women, much less sleep with them!"

"Bishop Weber, why can't the law enforce their own laws and clean up the prostitutes and these drug hoodlums?" Michael stared, unsmiling, at the red face bishop.

"Yeh, Weber, I don't care to get creamed by my woman over a bunch of whores!" James' face turned red with discuss "I mean, I would never touch another woman besides my babe anyway!"

"And Scott is a preacher, for the love of Mary! Man, this

is not hip!" Michael moved in his chair to keep his obvious anger from showing.

"Now boys, I think you can handle your women." Henry laughed nervously "As well as those overly sexy broads in Greystone. No one expects you to actually sleep with the harlots."

"You mentioned Greystone?" Gene slammed his fist on his seat "Just where the hell is Greystone?"

"Greystone is a small western town in Texas." The bishop swallowed nervously.

"And what are we supposed to be, cowboys?" Scott stared into the bishop's eyes "Tough ass, horny, no count shoot-em up cowboys!"

"Maybe Matt Dillion, old Doc and Chester!" James laughed, trying to picture Gene Scott as Matt Dillion.

"More like Butch and his hole in the wall gang! Real law breakers!" Michael frowned "Well Weber, which is it?"

"More like rich oil men!" Weber sit up, happy his companions had cooled down a little "Scott will be Clint Walters, a wealthy oil tycoon. Every place he buys, he hits oil!"

"Our boss, Mr. Clint 'Lucky' Walters!" Michael laughed "Everything he touches turns to oil!"

"Good! He can touch those prostitutes and turn them to oil, then we would be safe!" James patted Gene's back "Right boss man?"

"What are these two goons' names and what are their jobs?" Gene smiled at their solemn faces.

"Michael is Dave Jackson and James is Jim Collins, your trusted helpers and bodyguards." Weber looked pleased with himself until he heard Scott grunt.

"Henry, helpers? Bodyguards? Do I look like I need a damn bodyguard, especially these two? I should be their bodyguard."

"Scott, you are 'Lucky' Clint Walters and that's final!"

Weber arched his eyebrow. "Make it work!"

"Alright, if that's the way it is!" Gene Scott slapped his two friends playfully on their backs "My old trusting bodyguards, Dave 'Bullseye' Jackson and Jim 'Hot Shot' Collins, named after Lucky's favorite drink!" Gene slapped Henry Weber on the back nearly knocking him out of his seat. "Tell me Henry, where is this rich oil man going to live and where the shit is he going to get all his money?"

Weber reached inside his brief case and pulled out a large bag filled with cash, legal looking papers, and bank deposits.

"Here is your cash Lucky, more where that came from should you need it. Mr. Walters has a new bank account opened in Greystone Federal, with credit cards and checking. He has accounts at all the local shops and stores for his convenience."

Gene grabbed the bag out of the bishop's hand "Where did you get all this cash Weber? Rob a bank?"

"Scott, Scott." The bishop forced a smile at Gene's little joke "The church is working with the Fed on this mission. The finances are coming from both sources."

"Henry, that takes us back to the question, why us?" Scott slammed the heavy bag down on the floor. "This job is for the F.B.I. to handle, not a small group of missionaries!"

"Scott, the church and the fed want you. They have seen your work and are impressed with how you handle yourself. In short Scott, you get things done." Unwrapping another candy bar, he started eating "Scott, you are not just a missionary, you're…well…"

"You kick butt, man!" Michael patted his big friend's arm.

"Mike's right, Scott, I think you are the right cat for the job! Nobody can get a job done like you man!" James smiled up at the tough preacher who was taking in all the compliments. "I sure wouldn't want you coming after me, big fellow!"

"And besides Scott, these women of immoral acts, are

sinning against God. Maybe you could…you know…? Henry Weber blinked when Gene Scott rose out of his seat and pulled him up.

"And what Weber? Knock some sense in them? Kick the devil out of their rotten soul?" Gene laughed out as he slapped the startled bishop on his back, causing him to swallow his candy. "Relax old man! You are right! I am the best damn man for the job!" he smiled broadly at Michael and James who sit grinning from ear to ear. "And with my trusty side- kicks, how could things go wrong! Right fellows?"

"Damn right Scott! They won't see us coming!" Michael threw his legs on the empty seat beside him "Where do we live Weber? Care to fill us in?"

"That is what these papers are for." The bishop held up the legal documents and Gene Scott grabbed them out of his hand.

"Let me do the honors fellows, before our fine bishop drives us crazy. One is a deed to a two- thousand- acre ranch." Gene's eyebrow flew up "Isn't that a bit much, Henry?"

"Not for 'Lucky' Clint Walters!" Weber laughed, but stopped short from Scott's serious stare "There is a large ranch house with eight bedrooms, located in the middle of the property. It came up for sale at the exact right time for our mission. Mr. Walters' master bedroom is extra-large with an oversize king bed, for what you need. You know, action!"

"Action, Weber? I will action your fat mouth!" Scott grew irritated knowing he would gladly put that big bed to use if his Susan were with him and there would be plenty of action. "Why would we need so many bedrooms anyway? Are we planning to run our own whore house, Weber?"

"Scott, it's just for status. You know, Lucky, big man, big house." The nervous bishop started to put another piece of candy in his mouth, but Gene Scott slapped it out of his hand.

"If you don't stop eating candy Weber, I won't have to knock your teeth out! They will rot out all on their own!" Gene opened the other document in his hand "This is a permit to

28

drill for oil!" he stared down at the bishop "You don't really expect us to drill for oil?"

"It's just a front Scott! Where is your imagination?" Weber's eyes fell down on his last candy bar, lying on the dirty plane floor.

"My imagination Henry? I left it back in my childhood, when I had to grow up before most kids cut their permanent teeth!" Scott spoke loudly "What are we supposed to do about those sorry prostitutes?"

"This is no ordinary whore house fellows. These so call Ladies, are rented out to wealthy men for large amounts of money. The client can choose to stay in the twenty- room house in town or the gentleman can take these ladies to any of the fancy hotels in Greystone. If the client lives near the town, they may take them to their place." Weber wiped his brow as he watched the serious faces listening to his every word "Most of the gentlemen retain the same lady over a period of time. If they grow tired of their choice or feel they are performing badly, as not to suit their needs, they can switch them for another hooker."

"And you know all of this and nothing has been done to shut the place down?" Reverend Scott looked serious "Are these prostitutes the ones selling the drugs?"

"Our sources have informed us that the drugs are coming from within the whore house." Taking his handkerchief from his shirt pocket, Henry Weber wiped the sweat from his forehead. "We need to catch these women in action! This is a big operation, fellows, and most of the town is involved, including the local law enforcement! They target strangers, new to the area. Mostly rich men, very rich men!"

"You said we need to catch these women in action!" James swallowed "How are we supposed to catch prostitutes in action? Are we to take one of the hookers and do what they will be expecting and not get caught? Ali will kill me!"

"Look Hot Shot, there are ways to make a bitch believe

you gave her the best damn sex she has ever had and not touch her sorry ass!" Gene stared out the plane window "I'll fill you in later but for now partners, we are about home to our nameless ranch." He rolled his eyes over at the bishop.

"The name? I got it, the Lucky C Ranch, that will fit perfect!" Weber laughed "I will have Martin replace the old one with that!"

"Martin? Weber, the last thing I need is that coward George Martin in my hair!" Scott's temper flared "What the shit were you thinking, choosing Martin? He will be praying for our worthless souls when we bring those whores back to the ranch!"

"Now Scott, you can explain to brother Martin what you will be doing. I am sure he will understand and play along." Bishop Weber fastened his seatbelt when the light came on "Just buckle those seat belts and stop worrying. Martin will be a big help in your set up. He will be acting as your help, cook, butler, etc." he tried to smile normal "Just keep him away from the prostitutes. I'm not sure brother George would know what to do with them."

"Bishop Weber, I do not think I need to worry. George is hired help with low wages. He has a big house to run." Gene frowned "All by himself! God help us if he tries to reform them!" he laid back and prayed.

Chapter Six

Susan sat staring at the blank sheet of paper in front of her. How could she write a letter to her grandfather in Africa when her mind stayed on her husband away on a secret mission. Giving up, she lay her pen down and picked up a picture of her and Gene, together and happy. Her stomach floated with butterflies just looking at his handsome face. The telephone rang out and setting the frame down quickly, Susan dashed down the steps calling back

"I'll get it Pogo! It's probably Gene!" reaching the phone on the third ring, she picked it up "Gene?"

"Susan!" his voice came over the telephone clearly "How's my girl? Missing me already?"

"Oh Gene, it seems like I have been waiting forever!" she wanted to jump through the phone and grab him. "Where are you, sweetheart?"

"We landed in Texas a few minutes ago, little darling. That's where my assignment is." Gene laughed softly "My partners, Dave Jackson and Jim Collins, are getting us a car to drive to this small, out of the way, no name town, full of mining men. Just a bunch of rough and rugged rednecks!" he laughed "Nothing your old man can't handle."

"I know you can do anything you set your mind on darling." Susan longed to kiss his lips "This Dave Jackson and Jim Collins are new guys, aren't they?"

"Just new to us, Susan. They have been working undercover for some time." Gene smiled to himself and thought "Under the covers with Jackie and Ali." Then he said "They seem to be great guys, sweetheart. I know we will get along just find. Nothing for you to worry that sexy little head about. As for our job, it's a piece of cake." Gene bit his lip, knowing he had to lie about the real mission. "Just some drug pushers to flush out and get the ringleader."

"So, can I come?" Susan closed her eyes, hoping for the best.

"Sweetheart, it will be better if you stay at home. This bunch of men could get rowdy when they start drinking after leaving the mines. A pretty little thing like you might set them off. Instead of doing my job, I would be knocking the crap out of every miner in that worthless town." Gene spoke softly "And besides, if you were here I wouldn't be able to concentrate on my job at all. The faster I get done, the faster we leave this place."

"Gene, you said, no name town. Surely it has a name." picking up another picture of Gene, Susan clutched it next to her chest. There was no sound from the other end and her heart started pounding, afraid she had lost the connection. "Gene, are you still there?"

"I'm sorry sweetheart, Dave and Jim have got the car waiting in front and they are motioning for me. I got to run." Gene squeezed his eyes shut for lying again to the one he loved more than life.

"Can you call me again, darling?" Susan held her breath.

"I'm not sure what we will find when we get there, Susan. If they have any phones at all, they probably won't work, worth a shit! I can probably call when we stop for gas, sweetheart, if they have a public pay phone."

About that time, Michael and James drove up blowing the horn in a big Mercedes. James whistled out to Scott "Cool wheels, right Lucky?"

Gene motioned for the guys to get quiet and stared down at the receiver "Susan, the guys must have got tired of waiting and have pulled our rental right up beside me, so I better run."

"Gene, who is Lucky?" Susan looked puzzled.

"Lucky? Oh, you thought he was referring to a person, darling. What Jim really said was, cool wheels, right, we're lucky!" Gene paused, but Susan didn't come back with more questions. He was getting nervous "You know, like lucky to find the right kind of car to fit our character." Before Susan might come up with another question, Gene quickly added "Kiss the kids for their papa and tell Pogo to watch out for holes."

"Holes? What kind of holes are you referring to Gene Scott?" Susan frowned down at the receiver.

"It's just a running joke between me and my old pal, Pogo." Gene grew serious "Susan, I love you with all my heart and remember, you can always trust me."

"I do trust you Gene and I love you too, with all my heart, darling."

"Don't forget to say your prayers." He blew her a kiss "Sleep tight and dream about me."

"Always!" Susan blew him a kiss and then the phone fell silent. She wiped away her tears and went back to writing her letter.

Gene laughed at big car sitting in front of him "This is supposed to make me look rich?" he pushed Michael over, out of the driver's seat and settled behind the wheel "Let's see what this baby can do!" Gene floored the gas pedal and took off down the highway.

Susan sat brushing her long black hair when she heard the doorbell ring. Sticking her head out the bedroom, she called down to Pogo.

"Pogo, if you're not busy, can you get the door?"

Pogo walked from the kitchen, drying his hands on a dish towel. He glanced up the steps mumbling

"If I'm not busy? No, if you don't call fixing the lunch and washing up my mess, nothing!" Pogo opened the door and smiled at their two beautiful visitors. "Jackie, Ali, what a lovely surprise!"

Without a word, the two friends pushed passed Pogo and looked around the empty entry hall briefly then turned to face Pogo.

"Where is he, Pogo?" Jackie snapped.

"Where is who, Jackie?" the young man looked confused.

"Gene Scott! That's who!" Ali answered loudly as Susan made her way quickly down to see what all the commotion was about.

"Jackie, Ali, what's wrong? Why are you looking for Gene?"

"Because we are sure he knows where Michael and James are!" Jackie raised her voice as Susan tried to calm her down.

"Girls, I'm sure Gene has no idea where your fellows are. Gene is not even home. He has been called away on another mission."

"Oh! That James Tabor, I knew he was acting strange!" Ali stomped her foot.

"Yes, the very nerve of them two, sneaking off and lying about it!" Jackie's face flushed with anger.

"Girls, I assure you, Michael and James are not with Gene." Susan tried to smiled at her frowning friends "His partners are Jim Collins and Dave Jackson."

"A likely story! Those three are up to something and they don't want us to know!" Ali hit the coffee table and squinted her eyes in pain "Ouch! Damn men! I will kill James! I will kill all three of them!"

"Ali, you don't mean that!" Susan tried to take her arm, but she pulled away.

"Jim Collins? Ha, what a joke!"

"Dave Jackson! Most likely made up by some stupid amateur!" Jackie practically screamed.

"Jackie, Ali, there is no way Michael and James are with my husband!" Susan raised her voice in defiance "I trust Gene, he does not lie to me!"

"A…Susan?" Pogo pulled her to one side "They could be right."

"Pogo, have you gone nuts on me too?" Susan frowned at him.

Pogo pulled a crumbled piece of paper from his jean

pocket "I wasn't going to bother you with this, but now, I think maybe I should."

"Where did you get that trash Pogo?" Susan snatched it from his hand.

"Susan, it was in the bottom of Scott's trash can. When I emptied the trash this morning, it fell out." Pogo looked at her seriously "I think Scott was writing a message to Michael and James and he messed up this one."

Susan unfolded the crumbled piece of paper and began reading "Michael and James, Weber has called us on a mission somewhere. Don't know the details. Cannot bring wives, the place is not fit for ladies. Try to sne— Oh, Pogo, they are with Gene." Tears came into her eyes "Why did he lie to me?"

"Susan, I don't think he lied exactly." Pogo put his arm around her "I think he named their alias instead so their wives wouldn't find out."

"What have you got there, Susan?" Jackie took the note and read it aloud "I knew it! No place for a lady!"

"Who the hell said we were ladies?" Ali stopped, remembering what Scott had told them before "I say that you are ladies!' and she reflected on how good it made her feel. Ali calmed down and put her arm around Susan. "Sweetie, they're men, they don't think." She pulled Susan's chin up and smiled "Can you tell us where they went?"

"Gene said the two 'guys' were bringing their rental car around beside him, when he was talking to me at the airport." She sniffed "I ask him what the name of the town was and they interrupted our conversation, or…or so he pretended."

"Now Susan, you must not take this personal." Jackie tried to reassure her "Men do crazy things, thinking they are protecting us. We will just have to figure out where the devil they are."

"Gene did tell me they were in Texas." Susan sighed "The biggest state to track down three men that don't want to be found."

"What about Bishop Weber? We could make him tell us."
Ali frowned "If he can stop eating candy long enough to tell
us."

"It won't do any good to ask him. It was Weber's ideal not
to tell us in the first place. He will not tell us!" Susan looked
over at the front window when she heard a car pull up. Pogo
walked over and looked out to see who it was.

"Good Lord!"

"Pogo, who is it?" Susan took Jackie and Ali's hand.

"Miss wonderful redhead herself!" Pogo looked around at
the three friends and made a face "Gloria Ann Weber!"

Chapter Seven

Pogo opened the front door after Gloria Weber rang the bell. He forced a smile at the pretty redhead.

"Miss Weber, what a pleasant surprise. What do we owe the privilege for your lovely company today?"

"My goodness, Polard, how you have grown up." She pushed passed him, then turn back to face him "And you have went from boy to such a handsome young man." Gloria turned to smile at Susan who was observing her closely "You know handsome, if Gene can have a younger woman, I do not see why little bitty me can't fall for a younger man."

"Such flattery, Gloria, you must not get Pogo's hopes up like that." Susan teased, knowing Pogo would never go along with anything romantic with Gloria Ann Weber. "Is there a reason for your surprising visit?"

"As a matter of fact, there is." Gloria noticed Jackie and Ali standing just inside the family room, taking in the conversation "And just the other two ladies I need to talk to. All three of you, right here together! How convenient!" Gloria pushed passed Susan to join the interested party. Susan rushed in beside her and stood next to her friends, who were taking in the rude redhead.

"Let me introduce everyone." Susan nodded her head toward the redhead, who was obviously checking out the two unsmiling friends. "Ladies, this is Miss Gloria Ann Weber, Bishop's Weber's only child."

Jackie faked a grin "It's nice to finally meet you Gloria. Susan has told us so much about you."

Ali looked at her innocently "Yes, she has, like how you are still chasing after Gene, knowing he is a married man."

"I am well aware Gene is married. Very much so, I'm afraid." Gloria turned up her nose "Let me guess, you are

37

Jackie and Ali, short for Allison I assume?"

"Yes Gloria, these are my dear friends, Jackie Sorensen and Ali Tabor." Susan placed a hand on each of her friend's shoulder as Jackie spoke up

"That would be Jackie Beason and Ali McDonnel." Jackie winked at Susan "We will fill you in later."

"Well, never mind names Gloria, why are you here." Susan faked a smile at the redhead "If you're here to see my husband, Gene is not here."

"Yes, I know Gene is not here Susan. Daddy sent him on another mission." Gloria walked around the untidy room, smirking at what she saw and thinking to herself "How does Gene darling put up with this mess?" she turned back to the interested faces watching her "Daddy tell me everything about Gene. I would bet I know more about this latest mission assignment far better than either of you."

"Gloria Ann Weber, do you know where our men are?" Jackie took hold of her tender arm "Speak up red!"

"Well! The very nerve!" Gloria's eyes flashed fire "Maybe I won't tell you anything, and believe me, I know plenty! Like every little dirty detail!"

"Gloria, sweetheart" Pogo took her hands gently "You must try and understand these ladies are upset. They need to know what is going on with their men."

"Very well Polard. You are a dear." Her soft hand rubbed his cheek, then she turned to face the women "Gene perhaps told you about the drugs involved, being sold." She smiled, knowing the big secret she was about to reveal would bring a reaction from the possessive women "But drugs are not the only thing that is for sale, ladies."

"Alright, you have got my interest. I like a good sale!" Ali smiled at Jackie.

"Not this one dear, women aren't permitted to shop for this merchandise." Gloria smiled triumphantly, knowing she was about to spill the beans on what their men were really up to.

"A very large prostitute house, selling themselves to wealthy clients!"

"Prostitutes?" all three girls spoke in unison.

"You are telling me, that Bishop Weber sent Gene to break up a prostitute ring selling drugs?" Susan set her jaw tightly "What kind of damn mission is that for a minister?"

"Susan darling, your husband is no ordinary, run of the mill, minister." Gloria laughed "He is Gene Scott, for God sake!"

"Gene can take care of himself, Susan." Pogo put his arm around her trembling shoulders "Remember back when Scott was picked to break up the drug ring in TarSa? He had to make Mr. Big's girlfriend approve of him before he hired him."

"Really! Just what did Scott have to do, Pogo?" Susan grew loud.

"Scott was supposed to get her approval after having sex with her." Pogo held Susan tight as she bawled up her fist "Nothing happened Susan, relax! Scott is smart! He got her drunk and tricked her into believing they had great sex." Pogo laughed as he remembered "That Scott, the bimbo fell head-over-heels and he nabbed Mr. Big and the rest of the gang because of it!"

"Well, before I kill him, I will let him explain why he never told me that part about his undercover work!" Susan jerked herself free from Pogo, but he pulled her back and looked down at her seriously.

"As I recall Susan, you were leading on that college freshman. What was his name? Oh yes, Randy Sumner, same fellow who befriended Scott and sold him drugs. You really had Randy hot for you and you too was just doing your job to catch the bad guys."

Susan relaxed and smiled "You're right, Pogo. Gene loves me and only me. I trust him with all my heart and I'm all he needs…" she glanced at Gloria, who had been taking in their conversation with interest "Or wants!"

"Can I please go on?" Gloria flopped down on the sofa "Do you have any wine around here?"

"I could use some wine myself, if you have any, Susan." Jackie was getting impatient with Gloria Weber

"Pogo, go get three glasses of chardonnay for the ladies and grab yourself a beer." Susan patted his shoulder "I will have a bottle water. The twins will be up soon."

"Hold up until I get back! I don't want to miss a single detail!" Pogo left for the drinks. After everyone was seated and drinks had been served, Gloria continued.

"Jackie and Ali, I suppose you might be wondering who sent you that note assume to be from Michael, asking you to bring a picnic lunch to the building sight. They wrote they had a few hours off, something about someone going after more building supplies. When you arrived, there was nothing being built or no sign of your men."

"It was you! You wrote that note!" Ali set her glass down "You wanted us to find out our men were not there!"

"Very smart thinking, Mrs. Tabor." Gloria smiled knowingly "Oh, that's right, you're not married! It's Miss McDonnel!"

"Just why would you want us to know they were not there, Miss Weber?" Jackie did not like this arrogant woman.

"Because, Miss Beason, it is not right for your two men to run off like that, behind your back without telling you the truth!" Gloria let out a sigh "Men are so cruel and selfish." She smiled over at Pogo who stood propped up on the fireplace mantle. "Not you Polard darling, you are an exception." Gloria noticed all three women were staring angrily at her. She laughed nervously "They all have undercover names and occupations. Gene darling is Clint Walters, a rich oil baron. James is Jim Collins and Michael is Dave Jackson. They are Clint's bodyguards and pals. Reverend George Martin is the cook, butler, and housekeeper."

"Martin?" Pogo looked at Susan and laughed out "Boy oh

boy! I bet your old…I mean, your father, got an ear full from Scott over that bit of revelation. I bet the bishop's ears are still ringing!"

"Why, in the name of God, did your father choose George Martin?" Susan stood up "Martin will be trying to save everyone's soul, including good old Clint! He will give them away before they get started!"

"And who had the stupid ideal to put one man in charge of everything? If Clint Walters is as rich as you say, he would have a staff of workers, not one ridiculous man!" Jackie shook her head, trying to picture one man doing all the jobs in what had to be a big mansion.

"Now Susan, first of, Daddy did have a long talk with George." Gloria finished her wine and stood, making a distasteful face over what appeared to be cheap wine. "I am sure brother George knows to stay out of Gene's way." Her green eyes fell on Jackie "As for the work arrangement, the big house is just a statist cymbal of Clint Walters' wealth. He has no need of a full staff because all their activity will be done in town. He won't be having house guest!"

"What is this little town's name, as well as the whore house?" Ali joined the others slowly, feeling a headache coming on.

"The town is called, Greystone and the prostitutes' big mansion is simply named, Joe's Beauties." Gloria made her way to the front door "This prostitute business is much different from most red- light establishments. Every client gets to choose one 'lady', as daddy calls them, to do with as he desires. Those women will do 'anything' to make the rich customer happy." Gloria shook her red locks as though she disapproved their behavior. "The wealthy client can take one of the rooms at the brothel, or go to one of the many fancy hotels lining the street. If the gentleman lives nearby, he can take the hooker home for as long as he needs her service." She faked a laughed "And get this, if the customer grows tired of the broad he purchased, he can swap her in for another. It's all about money, ladies, and believe me, those overly sexy females cost a lot!" Gloria looked into Susan's angry eyes "It's when the client is really 'hot' over the bimbo, she hooks him on drugs, so even more money comes out of his pocket."

"Why hasn't the law in this sinful, worthless town, arrested the law breakers?" Jackie's voice grew angry "To think, my man is hanging around a bunch of trashy whores! I will strangle Michael as soon as I see him!"

"I think you need to teach them a lesson!" Gloria tried hard to keep a straight face. "I would show up and let him know whose boss! You will not get any help from the local police! They are all crooked as practically everyone living in Greystone."

"Show up and ruin your fathers well laid out plan?" Everyone looked at Susan in surprise and noticed her warm smile "I am sure we can trust our men, Gloria. I know I can trust Gene." She reached over and patted the startled redhead's arm "There is just one more thing you can share with us. Do you happen to know the name of good old Clint's ranch? To fool people, it must be something grand."

"Grand? Oh, yes, two thousand acres, called the 'Lucky C' Ranch." Gloria forced a smile and turned toward the front door "The very large ranch house has ten bedrooms to accommodate everyone. Three bedrooms for the men and three for the costly ladies, if they decide it's better to bring them there and get more undercover workers to come in. That leaves four extra bedrooms, if needed and staff quarters, where George will be, on the third floor, and the extra help, should they need them." Gloria laughed softly, knowing she had upset Jackie and Ali "Then I am off. What you choose to do is up to you. If it was my man, I would bring him home, away from all that temptation."

"Miss Weber" Pogo took her arm "might I escort you to your car?"

"Why yes, you certainly may, Polard dear and please call me Gloria." She batted her long eye lashes.

"Why thank you Gloria. I insist that you call me Pogo, like my close friends." He walked her out the door.

"That Pogo is a doll for getting that redhead out of this house!" Jackie let out her breath.

"And he is a very good actor. I was almost convinced that he was being genuine." Ali smiled, glad to see the back side of Gloria.

"Pogo was taught by the best!" Susan sat down to wait for his return.

"Cool wheels! Red is my color!" Pogo patted her head.

"Pogo, you say the sweetest things." Gloria pulled his head down and kissed him "I will take you for a spin sometime!"

"That sounds swell, doll." He closed her door "Drive careful, wouldn't want anything to mess up that pretty little redhead!"

"You are truly a doll, a living doll!" she laughed softly and drove away.

Pogo touched his lips, remembering her kiss, then he wiped them off and made a face as he walked back inside. "Boy, I hope I am appreciated around here!"

All three girls walked over and hugged the blushing young man.

"You are the greatest, Pogo!" Susan kissed his cheek, followed by her two friends.

"Pogo, if I didn't have my James, I would grab you for my own." Ali winked at him.

"Ladies, this all sounds heavenly and I am truly flattered, but I prefer to live." Pogo smiled at the three beautiful women in front of him "It would be bad enough dodging James and Michael, but good Lord, Scott would plaster me to the wall!"

Chapter Eight

After they quit laughing, from picturing Pogo plastered on the wall, Jackie turned to Susan and hit her lightly on the arm.

"Just what was that Susan, telling that redheaded bitch we could trust our men? You act as though it is not bothering you that your husband is with a bunch of hookers!"

"Jackie's right! I was just about to kick Gloria's sorry ass to the floor!" Ali stared at Susan "I don't get it, making miss high and mighty Weber think everything was alright with us!"

"Friends, going after our men was exactly the reaction Gloria Ann Weber wanted from us." Susan smiled "I just outsmarted her, that's all."

"Alright, I'll bite. How did you outsmart miss know it all?" Jackie sat down, pulling Susan down beside her.

"So, she could run to Gene and warn him about our finding out and that we were coming to stop them." Susan looked satisfied about her cleverness in seeing through the bishop's daughter's scheme "I simply outsmarted the fox, so to speak. Gloria's goal was to get us in trouble so the men would get upset with us and there could be a big argument."

"And that trashy redhead was hoping it would break you and Gene up!" Pogo grew loud "And to think she kissed me! Rats!"

The three girls looked up at Pogo smiling, just learning about the kiss. Pogo wasn't concern about the interested women watching him, he was too lost in his thoughts as he paced the floor thinking. As if a lightbulb flashed in his mind, he looked up and announced

"I have come up with a brilliant ideal!"

"Don't keep us in the dark, Pogo. Are you going to let us in on this brilliant ideal?" Susan teased "Or is it about…Gloria?"

"Very funny Susan." Pogo motioned for silence "We will go to Greystone, but it won't be as ourselves!"

Jackie bent forward "Keep talking Pogo, I think this is leading to something!"

"I will go as a rich pimp from New York." He looked thoughtful "Perhaps British, I could use an accent."

"Like Jackie, she's from England and could coach you! So far, so good!" Ali winked at the other two girls.

"You three will be my hookers, top, high price hookers. We will go to that house of sin and offer our services, with the owner getting a small share of the payout."

"Pogo, you are priceless! Your ideal is brilliant!" Susan laughed "I know Gene taught you everything you know!"

Pogo smiled, proud of himself as he looked into the happy faces in front of him.

"Now ladies, we need some good catchy names that fit a prostitute. I know you will like this part. Go shopping and buy several sexy, trashy, outfits, lots of make-up, hair products, so you can pile your gorgeous hair high on those lovely heads." He laughed "Perhaps you can pick some clothes out for your handsome pimp. I will call around and find the nearest flight to this God forsaken town." He touched Susan's shoulder "Susan, you can call your parents and line them up to keep the twins." He winked at her happy smile "They will love it, especially Mildred."

"They will love to keep them. I'll tell mom and dad, Gene called and said he needs us and it will be perfectly safe." Susan stood up laughing "This sounds like fun!"

"Fun maybe, but very serious." Pogo frowned "Gene will not be happy to see you dressed like a whore or me as a pimp, and neither will Michael and James, ladies! I am certain they will be mad as hell for a while." Pogo turned around, laughing "But it will pass when those fellows get you hookers in their bed!"

"Pogo, you are both clever and cute!" Ali kissed his cheek. "You are a living doll!"

"You are the second one to say that today." Pogo blushed as the three friends smiled knowingly "One more thing before you ladies hit the shops. I am sure good old Clint will insist on bringing 'his' lady to his house, as will Dave and Jim. I will inform Mr. Walters that I am your boss and I remain with you, in separate bedrooms of course. We got to keep the customer happy." Pogo swept his hand toward the front door.

"Go ahead and start shopping. I'll research some good names for us and find out a great price to offer the owner of the prostitute house." He kissed Susan "Don't worry about Samson and Delilah, I watch those little Scotts when they wake up from their nap."

"Pogo, you are the best!" Susan hugged him, grabbed her bag and dashed out behind Jackie and Ali.

Gene Scott pulled the Mercedes up at the gas pump and climbed out, stretching.

"Boy, that feels good!" he got some money from his wallet and handed it to his two companions "Listen up, fellows. I am going to the john and over there to that pay phone to make a call. Hot Shot, you go inside and get us some snacks for later, drinks and ice for our rented cooler. Bulls eye, fill up the tank!"

"Are you going to call Susan again, so soon?" Michael undone the gas cap "An attack of conscious, Lucky?"

"Something like that." Scott laughed "I will tell her just what she needs to know." He patted Mike's back "Who knows, I just might make things better for you and James, if those wives of your catch on to your made- up story and call Susan for answers."

"You are a good man, Lucky." James laughed and started into the convenience store calling over his shoulder "Maybe Ali won't kill me now."

After relieving himself, Gene came from the men's room and made his way to the payphone on the outside. He quickly noticed it was occupied by a little grey- haired lady, wearing a bright hat and red frame glasses. She was chatting, non-stop.

"A knee operation? Oh my, no my dear. Hazel Smith told me, only yesterday, Miss Helen went in for her kidneys, not a knee operation, Bertha."

Gene walked up and gently touched her shoulder "Excuse me, young lady." She looked up to find Gene Scott spread on a perfect smile "I hate to interrupt your conversation, but I really need to use the phone."

She smiled up at him warmly "Oh, I'm sorry young man." The elderly woman checked him out "My, my, aren't you handsome."

"Thank you, miss." She blushed as Scott kept smearing on the charm "I wouldn't bother you but, this call is somewhat of an emergency."

"Oh, gracious me!" she winked at him and lifted the receiver up to her ear "Bertha dear, this very polite and handsome young man must use the phone." Listening to the other party, she nodded her head "Oh, my yes, Bertha! He could be an actor for all we know."

Gene gently took the receiver from her hand "Permit me beautiful." Gene smiled down at her bright red hat "Lovely hat, nice color." She glanced down nervously, then rolled her eyes up shyly as he turned his attention to the other female holding up the line "Bertha? I hope you don't mind if I call you Bertha?" he smiled down at the old woman in the red hat "Yes, of course Bertha. Your lovely friend will call you back. Good day, Bertha." Gene hung up and started to dial Susan when he noticed the woman was still standing there, smiling.

"Would you mind, sweetheart, this is a personal phone call." Gene forced a smile.

"Oh, gracious me, of course. I'll just go inside and buy my bread." Her eyes crinkling under the red frame glasses, she started backing toward the store door "I hope to see you before you leave." She smiled and walked inside. Gene quickly dialed the number as he mumbled

"Not if I see you first, grandma!" he turned his back toward the store as he heard the recorder come on.

"Hi! You have reached Gene and Susan's! Please leave us a message! Thanks!"

"That's my girl." He smiled and whispered to himself "Maybe a message from me will be easier A little sweet talk to lighten up my guilt." Then he heard the peep.

"Susan, sweetheart, it's Gene! I'm sorry I missed you. I guess you've gone to the park with our kids or something. I am calling darling because I didn't like the way I left things the last time I called. I didn't exactly tell you everything I knew, although parts of it, I did. Remember the two fellows helping me, Jim and Dave. Well the truth is, that is their undercover names. You know them pretty well and I know my smart girl can figure it out. If those two lovely female friends of ours call asking questions about their husbands, tell them old Gene has their back and I'm teaching them everything they need to know to stay out of trouble.

The drug ring is one problem, the other job, well…" he swallowed "Weber was right sweetheart, it is something a lady should not have to deal with or know for that matter. Susan, darling, it is for your own good I cannot tell you all the details, but I am asking you to trust me." Gene closed his eyes "Darling, I love you, only you and you are the only woman I ever need or want, in every way. Keep the bed warm for me. I will be home as soon as possible." Gene checked his pants pocket and found one dime left "Sweetheart, my change is running out here. I will try to call you tomorrow, but after that, it could prove tricky. Got to go Susan. I love you, darling." The operator came on the line, please deposit another 25 cents and after a while the phone went dead. Gene held the receiver, staring at it and thinking to himself

"If I could crawl through this thing to Susan, I would instantly! Damn, I miss that girl!"

"Hey Lucky, are you going to stare at that phone forever?" James had walked up behind him "Can't get enough of that little gal of yours?"

"Very funny Hot Shot!" Gene slammed the receiver back in place "Did you get everything we need?"

"Right on man! That is, everything but our women!" James patted the big man's arm as they walked back to the car "That's alright Scott, we all miss our women."

When they reached the car, Michael was filling up the cooler "Scott, James tells me you got an admirer in the store." Michael laughed "some little grey hair grandma telling other women in line behind James about the handsome devil who borrowed the phone."

Gene looked through the store window "Oh shit, is she coming out?"

"There was a long line behind me Scott, but she was getting close to the checkout when I came out with our bags." James laughed at Scott's reaction "Whoops, here she comes!"

"Quick, in the damn car!" Scott whispered loudly as he dived in the back seat and laid down. "You can drive Mike! James in the front seat!" Gene could hear the elderly women calling out.

"Oh, young man? Has he already gone?"

"Michael, floor this baby and get the hell out of here!" Gene mumbled as the two friends in the front, laughed at the situation, then Michael speeded off down the Texas highway. He looked up in the rearview mirror at the tall preacher lying in the back seat.

"We are safe now, Scott. You can relax."

"Good!" Gene relaxed and closed his eyes "Drive safely and try to keep it down up there! I'm going to take a nap" He smiled to himself as he thought "and dream about Susan!"

Chapter Nine

The girls got out of their car laughing at all their packages. Jackie looked down at the little beagle that ran up carrying a small ball. Wagging its tail, the beagle dropped the ball at her feet.

"Hello cutie, want to fetch?" she bent down and retrieved the ball, then threw it across the big lawn. Jackie laughed softly as the little dog took chase "What a precious beagle."

"Poor Shags, I have been so busy today, I forgot to walk him." Susan got down and patted the small dog when it ran up to her and dropped his ball. "Shags, good boy! We will get Jobi to watch you while we are gone. Would you like that boy?"

Shags let out a yep and wagged his tail happily as though he understood. Susan smiled as he rolled over so she could rub his stomach.

"There you go boy! Pogo will bring you a treat!" Susan stood up and gathered her bags then opened the front door. "Gene will kill me for buying all these slutty clothes."

"Who knows Susan, he might have you wear them in your bedroom." Jackie laid down her large stack of bags. "I know Michael will get turned on with my selections."

"That little red number I bought will send James over the edge!" Ali fell, exhausted, on the sofa. Pogo made his way quietly down the stairs.

"Girls, can we keep it down, there are totters in the den playing on the floor! It took me an hour, on my knees, getting them interested in their toys! If they hear you in here, they will be under our feet, wanting all the attention. I got them fed and they were content when I carried a load of laundry upstairs to put away!"

"Thanks, Pogo." Susan smiled as she listened to her children playing peacefully. "You are a good god-father."

Pogo found a chair and sat down with his list of information. "Susan, there is a call for you on the answering machine. I think it was Scott. I was feeding the twins and couldn't get it."

"Thank you Pogo!" Susan raced up the steps, whispering loudly "I will be back soon!" she sat down next to the machine "Damn, I hate I missed Gene's call." She switched it on and listened closely to his every word. When he had finished, she smiled through tears. "He does care about how I feel. Oh God, I love that man!" Susan stared at the phone "We will probably be gone when he calls back. I have got to leave him a message!" she set the machine on unlimited message time and mashed the button.

"Hi, this is Susan. If this call is from someone besides my husband, please respect my privacy by hanging up and trying again in a few days, when you get my regular message. Thank you for understanding. Gene darling, I am so sorry I missed your call. It nearly broke my heart. You don't know what it means to me that you called and told me what you could. I really feel loved, my dearest Gene. I do trust you, more than you know, as you may trust me, sweetheart. I guess you are wondering why I left this message instead of being here to talk to you in person. It is something I am doing for the family. The twins will have a good time and little Shags will even be included.

Gene, my love, I will do more than keep our bed warm. I will keep myself 'hot', just for you! Who knows, we may be together sooner than we think! I love you, my wonderful husband and you are the only man I need or want!" Susan snapped off the machine and took a breath as she picked up a framed picture of Gene. "I am doing this for our family, Gene Scott, yours and mine! If there is any broad in bed with you at the Lucky C Ranch, it had better be me!"

Susan listened to her message one time and smiled an approval, got up and went downstairs to join the others.

"Did Scott share any more information with you, Susan?"

51

Jackie was going through her bags, lifting up different outfits. "As a matter of fact, Gene was quite wonderful!" Susan smiled as she opened one of her boxes "He even same as told me Michael and James were Dave and Jim. You have nothing to worry about girls, Gene is going to keep them in tow."

"Maybe, but drinking and wild women do not mix!" Ali squinted her eyes, uncertain of any man's ability to withstand a half -naked woman making over him.

"That is why our flight leaves tomorrow around 10:00 a.m." Pogo stood up smiling and noticed Susan's questioning eyes "And yes Susan, your parents are coming over in the morning to get the twins and Shags!"

"You have certainly been the busy one, Pogo. Did you come up with our names, as well?" Jackie stood up and started getting her bags repacked.

"I certainly did, Miss Tracy Evans!" Pogo opened the notebook he had been holding "I am Priencel Stevenson, from London."

"What kind of name is Priencel, for heaven's sake?" Ali laughed out as the other two girls joined in.

"A very distinguish name! As a matter of fact, Sir Priencel was knighted by the queen herself, some forty years back!" Pogo cleared his throat as the three girls laughed harder "Surely, you heard something about him, Jackie?"

"No, I'm sorry, Pogo darling." Jackie tried to keep a straight face "I'm sure I would never forget a name as unusual as Priencel, but then the queen and I aren't exactly bosom friends and she has made many a good citizen a knight."

Pogo shook his head as he continued "Susan, you are Roxanne Sander and Ali is Monica Haywood. Tracy, Roxanne, and Monica, are my undercover girls!" he laughed and noticed the girls had stopped laughing "Girls, you know, undercover?"

The girls broke into more laughter as Jackie headed toward the door.

"We are just pulling your leg Pogo. Those are good names, even for hookers, to do their 'undercover' job! Now we must run, pack and be ready to get back here early in the morning."

"I am going to enjoy this little acting gig." Ali loaded her packages in the car "And it comes with benefits!"

Susan suddenly remembered they weren't married and ran out to stop them.

"I just remembered your last names!" What gives? Are you not married?"

"Your husband, my dear, is a minister and one that does not approve sex without marriage." Jackie smiled as she climbed into her car "Gene Scott would never approve of us living together, but that's the way we all prefer it."

"Scott started calling us their wives in Africa, so we played along to keep the peace." Ali laughed, remembering the handsome preacher calling her Mrs. Tabor. "Poor innocent man, hasn't caught on to our actual living arrangements."

"I'm sure not going to tell him." Susan laughed "We had to get married before Gene would have sex with me. Now we are making up for lost time."

"If I have said it once, I will say it again" Jackie turned on the motor "you are one lucky girl, Susan!" waving, they drove away as Susan watched them drive out of sight.

"Yes Jackie, I am the luckiest girl alive!" she turned and raced inside to pack.

Chapter Ten

Reverend Gene Scott pulled the Mercedes up to the gas pump, one last time before reaching their destination, the Lucky C Ranch. After switching off the motor, he looked at his companions.

"Alright boys, this is the last service station until we get 'home'." The three men decided to drive around the town of Greystone to avoid anyone in town from seeing them until they could change into more convincing clothes. Once there, their new wardrobes would be waiting for them.

"Michael, fill up the tank, James, go inside and buy beer, wine, and liquor, if they sell it. You can bet your sweet butt Martin did not get any." Scott got out and looked around until he spotted a payphone, just on the end of the building. "I will be making a call."

"Calling Susan again?" Michael started filling up the big tank "Wish I could call Jackie."

"Mike, you know very well, your woman has a stubborn streak." Gene laughed "You know she would be on the next bus out here and we do not need our women around these whores!"

"Yes, you are right. Go and make your call." Mike faked a smile and turned back to his job as Gene chuckled.

"I'm glad you see it my way, pal." His eyes fell on the empty phone booth "I better get over there fast before some gossiping granny shows up." Walking over quickly, he dropped some money into the slot, grateful he had made change at the café they had lunch at. After dialing, he got the answer machine again and heard Susan's message, asking people who called to call back, because she was leaving a message just for him. He closed his eyes and whispered

"Shit! This could mean a cursing out or…" his eyes lit up

with mischief "some "hot' sexy talk." Gene was listening closely and hadn't noticed James stepping up behind him.

"Scott, do you always stand and stare at a telephone?"

Gene put his finger up to his lip for silence and mumbled "Will you stay quiet, Tabor!"

"Oh, I get it. Susan is letting you have it! She is telling you off!" James shook his head.

"Look buddy, I'm going to let you have it if you don't shut the shit up!" Scott whispered loudly "It's a recorded message, dummy! Now get quiet!" Gene listened to the last romantic words and laughed lazily.

"Just wait until I get home my little darling! We will make that bed warm together!" Gene gently put the receiver back on the hook.

"Man! Sounds like we had better get this job done pronto, right Scott, baby?" James smiled slyly as he picked with the big man "I don't know how long you can wait before you can get under those 'hot' sheets with Susan!"

"Tabor, wipe that shit-eating grin off your face before I knock it off for you! Now move to that car before I kick your ease dropping ass all the way to my ranch!" Scott pushed passed him "You had better have bought plenty of booze, because after I get there with all my helpers, I'm going to need a stiff drink!" Gene walked over to the car and slung the door open.

"Want me to drive, Scott?" Michael forced back a grin from overhearing the conversation between James and Gene. "You have been driving ever since we left this morning."

"Right!" Scott left the door open and walked around to the other side "Tabor, to the back! I do not care to look at your cocky face for now! I'll ride shotgun!"

They rode off in silence and no one spoke a word until they pulled the expensive car to a stop in front of the large ranch house. James sat up as he looked at the rich estate.

"Shit! This thing is gigantic! Lucky, you have got one hell of a place here!"

"Yeh, Lucky, I knew you were rich, but damn, you must be loaded, man!" Michael quickly got into character.

Gene laughed loudly, feeling more relaxed, after his mad spell with James.

"Listen boys, old Clint Walters has more than you can count on your fingers and toes! Lucky is loaded!" Gene's attention was drawn to the massive front door opening and George Martin stepping out, hands on hips, looking angry. "Good Lord! It is our worthless partner, greeting us!" Gene gritted his teeth in aggravation. "I hope he hasn't done anything stupid! What was Bishop Weber thinking about letting Martin help us on this mission?"

Martin walked briskly out to meet them. "Reverend Scott, you are late! What took you so long? I was beginning to think I was going to have to bust the prostitute and drug ring all by myself!"

"You, Martin? Bust a ring of whores?" Gene looked over at his two partners trying hard not to laugh "Fellows, I ask you, can you imagine Reverend Martin busting this prostitute case? I suppose they might turn themselves in after all his caterwauling and praying for their worthless souls!"

"Or maybe the good town's people would hang old George out to dry!" Michael laughed as he patted the red face minister's back. "Better leave those hookers to us, Martin and stick to cooking and cleaning."

"Well, you see, that is what I did not understand." Martin took a step back when Scott started toward him, looking angry.

"There is nothing hard to understand, George! You are in charge of the damn house, period! Cleaning up the prostitutes is our job, get it?"

"Scott, there you go, misunderstanding my statement, as usual!" the shorter minister laughed nervously "I have no intention of getting near those harlots! It is my job description I am referring to, but I fixed the problem."

"Martin, I'm afraid to ask you this next question." Gene

closed his eyes, feeling a sense of dread at what he was about to hear. He got in the nervous minister's face "Just what have you done to fix your problem?"

"Mr. Walters, sir…" George tried to get into his role to avoid the rage building in the big man standing over him "It's simple really. A man of your great wealth and high standing, need a staff of servants, sir,

So, I took the liberty and hired a cook, a housemaid, and a garner."

"You did what?" Scott stormed out, expecting the worse and getting it "Martin, you damn idiot! What are you trying to do? Get us caught even before we start?"

"It just did not look right, one man doing the cooking and the cleaning in this giant house!" Martin looked up bravely "Besides, you need a butler and I can fill that position outstanding!"

"Boys, we are working with an idiot! A stupid, ridicules idiot!" Scott took Martin by his collar and lifted him off the pavement "We never intended for you to do all the cleaning and cooking around here, George! We were going to pitch in and help! We are only pretending to be rich and it's not like I am having the queen coming by for a damn visit!"

"But, those fallen women are coming here, will they not? They will expect you to give orders to your staff, which should actually be a whole lot bigger than four people." The red face minister took a breath of relief when Scott sat him down.

"Martin, where is this staff you hired? Are they here yet?" Gene looked around him "Well?"

"They will arrive today Scott. Be on your best behavior." George Martin turned up his nose and headed back inside, Scott and his companions right behind him.

"Listen Martin, you are just about to get on my bad side!" Scott growled "Just show us what you got, supplies, food, linens, rich clothes, and guns!" his eyes took in the fancy surroundings "And I'm sure you got plenty alcohol to drink."

"Alcohol! Heavens no, Scott! Brew is the devil's drink!" George jumped when Gene started toward him.

"Look Martin, we need plenty of 'devil's brew', to serve those scarlet women, you idiot!" Scott let his attention wonder around the room to keep from striking the irritating preacher "You do not expect us to take those broads up to our bedrooms sober, do you?"

"Good Lord Scott! I don't expect you to take them to your bed at all!" Martin swallowed "The very idea! Oh, dear Lord!"

"Martin, If I hear you start praying, you, sissy shit coward, it better be for God to spare your worthless life!" Scott yelled "I better not hear one word of prayer or bible talk come from that big mouth of yours! Remember, we are all heathen here and do not forget it! Now, where are the damn guns Martin, and there better be guns!"

"Guns? Yes, there are lots of guns" shaking, Martin pointed to the closed cabinet "The Feds stocked it up good. I hope you know how to use them."

"Maybe I will practice on you George!" Gene shook his head and grunted to himself "I have got to get a hold of myself! I am starting to act like old Lucky."

"Scott, what's with this hired help?" Michael checked out the assortment of firearms "Wouldn't the church or the Fed bring in their own people if they wanted more help? How can we trust strangers?"

"Mike's right! Weber said most of the town people were in on this crooked gang!" James stared over at George Martin who pretended to be busy straightening out a hall table. "What the hell where you thinking man? You are one stupid ass!"

"Feeling loved Martin?" Scott pushed the stiff man down on the sofa against the wall "You don't even realize what you've done, do you?"

"I…I only thought…" Martin swallowed, seeing the three serious faces staring down at him.

"That's just it Martin, you don't think things through!"

Scott's voice grew strong "We cannot talk freely around here now! We will have to keep our phony act up all the time around this staff you hired!"

"They're just hired help Scott. A cook, a housekeeper and…" before George could continue, Scott stopped him.

"Martin, they could all be spies! Damn spies for the leader of this crooked ring, reporting back everything they hear!"

"I never thought of that. They were all so perfect for their job and they came highly recommended." George forced a weak smile "I think if you met them…"

"Oh, I plan to meet them, Martin!" Scott yanked him to his feet "Tell me their names and all you know about each one."

"Vera Simon is a widow lady who will be our cook. She has a lot of experience in cooking and for a lot of men. The fine lady has seven children, all sons, grown and moved out. Mrs. Simon served me some of her dishes and they were quite wonderful."

"After eating your own cooking George, anything would taste wonderful to you." Scott looked over at Michael and James "Just to be on the safe side, we better take turns watching her in case she tries to poison us or slip drugs in our food."

"Really Scott, don't you think that going a step to far?" Martin laughed nervously and continued "The housekeeper is Miss Maxine Fletcher, an old maid who has worked for Mr. Roger Wilson and his wife, a rich banker in town and even for the mayor of Greystone, a Mr. Jessie Barker and his wife, Harriet. She stayed on with them for twenty years until he retired and moved into a retirement community.

"That's perfect George!" Gene Scott rolled his eyes up in discuss "I am sure you checked out her story." Knowing the scatter brain minister, Gene knew he had not check out any of their stories so he continued "The garner, let me guess, this talented ground keeper last worked for Joe's Beauties Whore House, correct?"

"Absolutely not! Very funny, Reverend Scott!" Martin walked over to the window facing the driveway and looked out, then checked his watch. "Horus Hampton was the grounds keeper for Greystone City Park for two years before he was let go."

"Shit! That is some experience!" Gene walked over next to Martin and looked out the window "Is there something out there, Martin? What time are those spies coming?"

Martin looked at his watch "They should be arriving in about fifteen minutes." Martin jumped when Scott yanked him around.

"I guess it's a good thing I am a quick -change artist!" Scott yelled "Hot Shot, you and Bull's Eye grab your luggage and make tracks up those steps!" Scott glared at George Martin "Martin, my room, the damn master, which one?"

"The first door on the right, Scott. James and Michaels are the two across the hall." The nervous preacher started to sit down but Gene yanked him back to his feet.

"It's Mr. Walters, Martin! If you call me Scott in front of those people, I 'will' kill you, understand? And from now on, you are Haywood! Do not let our real names slip out, got that! Now, wait on that 'staff' and have them wait for me if they are early!" Gene stormed up the big wide steps.

Chapter Eleven

Martin stood looking confident at the foot of the stairs when Gene appeared at the top.

"Mr. Walters, sir, would you like to view your help now?"

"Very good Haywood." Gene walked proudly down the steps. He was dressed like a western hot shot down to his leather cowboy boots. The handsome preacher took in the three strangers watching him descend the tall staircase. "I hear you will be working for me. My name is Clint Walters, the owner of this little spread. Haywood, would you introduce these fine folks?"

"Of course, sir." Martin motioned for the heavy-set woman with rosy cheeks and she stepped up next to him, smiling from ear to ear. "This lovely lady is Mrs. Vera Simon, a most excellent cook, sir."

"It is a pleasure to meet you Mr. Walters. I am truly grateful for this job sir. I was about to give up looking when I noticed the want ad in the Greystone Daily. It is truly a blessing." Her smile was bright and genuine.

"Haywood tells me you have seven sons, Mrs. Simon, and all grown up." Scott gave her one of his winning smiles "Now that's hard to believe Vera. You could pass for a schoolgirl yourself."

"Oh, my goodness, Mr. Walters!" she giggled "You are a charmer. A schoolgirl! I bet you flatter all the ladies, sir, with your kind words."

"Not all the ladies Vera, just the ones I like." Gene teased "I am sure you will do fine, as long as you cook as good as old Haywood brags and you do not try to poison me." He pinched her chubby cheek.

"Poison you? Never sir! I never use poison in my recipes!" Vera Simon laughed loudly.

"Then I thank you, young lady." Scott winked at her, then turned to George Martin and nodded toward the sour face woman observing his actions "Who is this lovely lady, Haywood?" Gene smiled at her stone face.

"This is Miss Maxine Fletcher, the housekeeper I told you about, sir." Martin's face was flushed from all Scott's comments to the chubby cook.

Maxine remained stiff as she spoke in a deep voice. "I beg your pardon, Mr. Walters, but you keep calling Mr. Martin, Mr. Haywood."

"That crazy Haywood!" Scott frowned over at the red-faced man who was giving him an I'm-sorry look "Martin is his first name, madam. He likes to sound casual at times, especially when it comes to lovely ladies, like you and Vera."

"I see." She remained cold and stone face "I am a very good housekeeper, Mr. Walters. I am very clean and very neat and that is how I choose to do my work, sir. I do not care to socialize with the other staff. I prefer staying to myself, sir. I'm a very private person."

"I understand." Scott tried not to laugh "Miss Fletcher, I like neat and I like clean, but you see, I really like a cheerful staff." He watched her drop her eyes toward the floor "Do you think you could squeeze a smile out of those luscious lips, Maxine?"

Martin almost got strangled as he began coughing. "She is clean and neat sir. I say as long as she does her job well, what's the harm if she wishes to be left alone?"

"Haywood, my dear fellow" Gene slapped Martin's back causing him to stumble forward "I think Maxine..." Gene smiled at her broadly "Your name slips off my tongue so easily. I may call you Maxine, yes?" she nodded a positive "I think you would have a beautiful smile if you just put forth a little effort." He lifted her chin "You do want employment here, am I correct?"

"Yes sir, very much." She spoke softly and gave him a small smile.

"Now, that didn't hurt you, did it?" Gene gently patted her shoulder "Keep up the bright smile Maxine! You're hired. Next!"

"Mr. Walters, aren't you going to ask Miss Fletcher is she is going to put pins and needles in your sheets?" Vera Simon giggled.

"Why Vera, I think someone who is as cheerful as Maxine would never dream of upsetting her boss." Gene laughed "You enjoy a good joke too, don't you Vera?"

"I do, Mr. Walters! The poison joke was so funny, I just thought of the pins and needles! You know, you climb into bed and…" she giggled loudly "you get the 'point'!" her chubby stomach shook when she laughed.

"Several points, dear lady." Gene laughed and noticed the quiet man stepping up in front of him and bowed slightly, then tried to stand straight.

"Sir, my name is Horus Hampton and I would be honored to be your garner."

"Horus, my dear man, there is no need for you to bow in my presence. I am not a damn king, just a rich, kick-ass oil man!" he checked out the thin, older man, standing slumped over, in front of him. "Horus, if you don't mind me asking, how old are you?"

"I do look a bit older than I am, sir. I will be fifty-eight on my next birthday, come October."

"Why did you get canned from your job at the city park after just two years?" Gene Scott found himself feeling sorry for this sad little man.

"I'm afraid I did get canned, as you put it." The garner looked down, feeling embarrassed "I do like to take a nip now and then." Horus quickly looked up to defend himself "But only after hours, mind you. Never touch the stuff while I'm tending to my duties, sir."

"Horus, my good man, me and the boys like to take a nip too. A little more than now and then!" Gene chuckled as he

63

patted the frail man's arm "Just keep my place looking great and you can enjoy your nip on your spare time. Are you from Greystone? You don't look like a Texan."

"Good observation Mr. Walters. I'm from Virginia and only moved here a little over two years ago." Mr. Hampton smiled warmly, already liking his boss "I was lucky to get that job over at the park ground and I was doing a fine job until them ladies in that fancy lady's club said I wasn't fit to work there. They complained to the city board that I wasn't keeping things pretty enough." He looked sad "It had to be the drinking, Mr. Walters."

"Then their loss is my gain!" Gene looked over the small group "Haywood will show you to your rooms. Please take the rest of today to get settled in and start to work first thing in the morning." Gene winked at Vera Simon "Sweetheart, I am an early riser, if I don't have a little filly to entertain, so I will have my breakfast around seven."

"Yes, sir and don't you worry, I am an early riser myself. Getting seven boys up, fed breakfast and off to school for so many years, has got me up and at-em, every day! I will fix you a good hardy breakfast sir." Vera smiled with confidence "Do you prefer your breakfast in bed or in the breakfast room, sir?"

"Defiantly the breakfast room, beautiful. I don't think I could control myself if you showed up in my room carrying a tray of good food!" Gene joined Vera in a hardy laugh as he noticed Martin's dropped jaw and big eyes "Don't say it, Haywood! Just do your job!" Scott gritted his teeth and started back up the stairs.

Chapter Twelve

Pogo pulled the rented red Lincoln Town car into Greystone. He glanced down at his watch, 2:00 p.m. Nervously he looked over at Susan sitting beside him. All three girls had really gotten into their parts and were dressed to the nines, like hookers, complete with lots of make-up.

"Pogo, does my lipstick need a touch up?" Susan opened her purse to find her mirror.

"Susan, if your lips get any redder, I'm going to start calling you cherry lips!" Grinning, he looked up into the mirror at the other two pretend prostitutes. They were busy casing the town while chatting away, not nervous at all. Pogo slowed the big car to a stop beside the street, then turned to face them.

"Ladies, it's not too late to turn back now. Maybe we will be in Scott's way, you know, to do his undercover work."

"Pogo, that word, undercover?" Susan frowned "If Gene Scott is going to do 'any' undercover work, it will be with me!"

"You tell him Susan!" Ali patted Pogo's back "Look Phil, we've come all this way to get this job and, we are staying, with or without our pimp!"

"She's right, Phil Priencel! Roxanne, Monica, and Tracy are tired of having 'no' sheet duty!" Jackie pointed at the big mansion down the street taken up a whole city block "I bet that is Joe's Beauty's. The big red door out front is a sign stating, gentlemen are welcome! From the looks of the size, I would say, there is plenty room for three more gorgeous hookers and their handsome pimp."

"Tracy is right, Phil! What do you say?" Susan patted Pogo's fidgeting leg. He smiled sheepishly.

"Forgive me ladies. I guess I got cold feet for a moment. I was seeing Scott's fist in front of my nose!"

The group joined in laughter as Pogo pulled the Lincoln

up in front of the massive mansion and climbed out.

"Come on girls, if I have the merchandise with me, I don't think big Joe will turn down my offer." Pogo knocked on the red door and stepped back when it opened and a well-dressed woman lathered in heavy perfume looked out. Her gaze fell on Pogo standing out in front, then quickly passed him to see the three glamorous women waiting behind him.

"How may I help you, young man?"

"Permit me to introduce myself, madam. My name is Phil Priencel from New York City and these three ladies are under my employment." Pogo lifted her perfumed hand and kissed it, then sneezed from the strong smell. The three waiting behind him tried to keep a straight face, although inwardly they were laughing. "You have a lovely place here, Miss?" Pogo watched her blush, making her cheeks even redder.

"It's Mrs. Stallington, young man. My husband is Joe Stallington, the senior owner of our establishment."

"Oh, you're married? Shame, my loss." Pogo felt Susan's light kick on his shin "Mrs. Stallington, may I introduce my girls, Roxanne Sanders, Tracy Evans, and Monica Haywood."

"It's nice to finally meet you Mrs. Stallington. My given name is Roxanne, but my close friends call me peek-a-boo." Susan's smile was radiant as she looked around "You have a lovely house."

"Thank you, Roxanne." She smiled and looked at Jackie "And you are Tracy?"

"Yes madam. I am called 'hot hips' by my regulars in New York. Such charming men and they tip really well." Jackie draped her arm around Pogo "Even though we have a big following back home, dear Phil wanted to take our 'act' out on the road."

"Our Phil always keeps things interesting. I am called undercover because that is where my clients know me." Ali reached around Jackie to shake hands with the older woman "Monica Haywood."

Pogo stood listening with his mouth open, as the three girls gave out their nicknames to the co-owner.

"Is there anything wrong, Mr. Priencel?" Mrs. Stallington stared at the red face young man.

"My dear Helen, I cannot blame this young man for gasping for air!' Big Joe Stallington walked down the fancy staircase, admiring the three beauties waiting below "I couldn't help hearing everything you said. Charming ladies you have got, Phil." Joe slapped Pogo on the back, as he smiled from ear to ear. "I may call you Phil?"

"If I can call you big Joe!" Pogo composed himself and stepped up.

"I wouldn't have it any other way, Phil. What can big Joe do for you, my friend?"

"The girls and I are taking their act on the road for a few months. We move around from town to town, selling our wares, if you will." Pogo laughed "It appears you have everything we offer sewed up in this lovely town. I thought we might work out a deal."

"Sounds like an interesting project, Phil!" he smiled as his eyes fell on Susan, Jackie, and Ali. The lusty owner could feel his pulse racing "Keep talking Phil, you have piqued my interest!" Joe's hand reached out and patted Susan on the butt "I do like them young."

"A…yes!" Pogo frowned at his behavior "If you don't mind Joe" Pogo walked in front of the three girls, as to block them from this brazen man's advances "These little ladies will be working for me big Joe, but I will give you a cut of everything we bring in. How does that sound?"

"So, you work here or wherever the client chooses and I will get…half!" Big Joe lit a cigar "Take it or leave it, Phil! My house, my town, my booze, my clients!"

"You drive a hard bargain big Joe. Let me talk it over with my girls." Pogo motioned the girls over to the side.

"Take it Pogo." Susan whispered. "We're not in this for

the money anyway, remember?"

"We've got our foot inside the door, now we just wait for our men to come shopping!" Jackie whispered.

"Pogo, let me take things from here." Ali motioned the group to follow as she walked up to the owner. "Joe, darling, we have talked over your proposal. If we stay here with a client, Phil stays. If we go somewhere with a client, Phil goes with us. We are like a big family, Joe, the four of us. But wherever we are, Phil knows to keep out of our way when we are working. He wants the customer to be 100% satisfied. He just remains close by in case we need him. You do understand, don't you, Joe darling?" Ali took the cigar from his hand and took a big draw, then blew out the smoke. "Mumm, my favorite brand!" she winked at him as she continued "As for paying us half, we girls think that is a fair price to ask. Your house, your town, your booze and all your rich clients! The tips alone will make up the difference!" Ali winked at a speechless Pogo "Phil was outvoted, but he finally gave in, right doll?"

"What can I say Joe? They are my working force! I've got to keep them happy!" Pogo held out his hand "Is it a deal?"

"How could I pass up such a great offer!" the wealthy man shook Pogo's outstretched hand. "You have arrived just in time! We have some very rich clients coming in late this evening. I will line your ladies up with mine!"

"That sounds terrific!" Pogo, forced a smile "I, of course, will give the final o.k. for my girls!"

"Great! Done and done!" Joe laughed loudly and ordered the maid to bring a bottle of champagne. After handing everyone a glass of the bubbly, the owner held up his glass "Let us toast our partnership, then you shall be shown to your quarters!"

The small group lifted their glasses in a toast as Susan whispered to Jackie "I hope the clients coming this evening are rich oil men!"

Chapter Thirteen

Gene Scott pulled his car to a stop in front of the huge house. He turned to face Michael and James, for last minute instructions.

"Alright fellows, this is it! We go in and make a deal with this big Joe for three weak looking girls and take them back to the ranch."

"And after we get there, we have a drink together in the great room, then take them upstairs to our bedroom." James stared at the wide front door "Why are the doors always red?"

"Never mind that, James!" Scott mumbled "We fill them up with lots of booze, laced with a sleeping pill, until they are passed out."

"When they come to, we lie about having some of the best sex we have ever had." Michael shook his head, unsure of the plan "Boy Scott, it's really going to be hard to lie about that one."

"Just make it work, Mike!" Scott climbed out and waited for his partners to join him "You know your woman gives you the best damn sex you have ever had, but this is what you call acting, Fellows. You have to sound convincing to these fallen women or they will see right through you." He made his way to the red door and whispered, "I swear, if George Martin starts praying for God to save us, just hold me back!"

James and Michael laughed as they followed their tall strong friend up to the stone stoop where he rang the bell and watched the same woman open the door and give them a big smile. Her bright red lipstick made her white teeth stand out as she motioned them inside. James lend over and whispered in his friend's ear

"I hope they all don't look like this one!"

Scott turned to give him an angry stare as he pushed passed him and whispered

"Will you cool it, damn it!" then Gene turned to the woman and smiled, sensing her trying to make out what they were discussing. He began to turn on the Scott charm "My dear lady, might I tell you how lovely you look this evening." The owner's wife blush as the handsome man continued "If you are going to be among the choice of ladies, it's going to make it difficult to choose."

"Oh, my...no, I regretfully say. "She stumbled with her words as her mind whirled at the thought of being in bed with this very handsome man "I am Helen Stallington, the wife of big Joe, the owner."

"I truly beg your pardon, madam, but it's a shame big Joe can't offer a hot broad like you!" Scott laughed, trying to drown down Michael and James' soft snickering. "Some like 'em young, some, middle age, but I like 'em all, even the 'hot' older models, like you darling, a real classic!"

"It does my heart good to see a man who appreciates the female sex as much as I do!" Big Joe stepped down the wide staircase.

"Ease dropping, are you, dear fellow?" Gene Scott smiled broadly at the robust man observing him and the boys. "You must be the big man himself, Joe."

"And you have to be Clint 'Lucky' Walters!" the owner shook Scott's strong hand.

"My sources tell me you are a very wealthy oil man! Why did you pick a small town like Greystone to find oil, Mr. Walters?"

"Please call me 'Lucky', big Joe!" Scott took the expensive cigar Joe offered "Great smoke Joe, one of my favorites!" after lighting it, he winked his approval, then continued "You ask me why I came to your small town. My people have done their homework, Joe. They find the land just outside of Greystone has a promising future in oil." Scott chuckled as he slapped the owner's back playfully, causing him to choke on his cigar smoke. After inhaling the good tasting tobacco and blowing out the smoke, Gene's eyes lit up. I can smell oil, Joe! It is out there on that two thousand ace spread! But" he shrugged his shoulders and laughed out "If it ain't out there, hell, I'll just pack up and drill someplace else! That's what I do, Joe, drill baby, drill!" Gene smiled back at his two quiet companions who had been taking in Scott's great acting. Gene walked around the fancy sitting room, looking over the expensive furniture. "The other thing I enjoy doing is riding a pretty sexy filly!" Gene's eyes fell on the owner "Well, Joe, where are you hiding all those little fillies?"

"The girls are getting ready for you and your companions, Lucky, but first, let's discuss the arrangements." Mr. Stallington motioned for a maid, dressed in a low cut, very short dress, to bring out the bar wagon. "We have different set ups here, Lucky and you may pick which one suits you. To stay here, in one of our rooms or any of the fine hotels in Greystone. You may also choose to take the lady home with you! The time she spends with you will be your decision." The owner past around glasses of champagne as he continued "Fellows, if you grow tired of the lady, you may switch her for another at any time." Joe held up his glass "If those arrangements agree with you, we may bring out the girls. Toast!"

Gene Scott clinked his glass to Joe's. "Toast, big Joe!" Gene chuckled "That is a damn deal the boys or I can't refuse!" he pulled a stuffed envelope from his shirt pocket, filled with one hundred- dollar bills, and handed it to the happy owner. "I checked your prices earlier and there is enough in here for the first week, with a little extra for the girl or girls I pick!" he winked at his companions "Plus, you will find plenty there for the boy's pick!"

"You are my kind of man, Lucky!" Joe smiled as he drank down his champagne and examined the large amount of money in his hand." Pay up front before collecting your gift!"

"That's because I'll be too damn tired to pay, after tossing around under the sheets with some sexy little…" Gene's jaw dropped as he watched Susan making her way down the middle of the wide staircase "a…a little…num…ber!" he couldn't take his eyes off his sexy dressed wife as she lined up with the rest of the provocative group of prostitutes.

"Lucky, my man, don't tell me you are at a loss for words!" Joe smiled at the line-up of sexy women, all alluring in their own way. "I bet you never dreamed we had so many beautiful ladies to choose from."

Michael and James gathered silently around Scott as they stared, wide-eyed, at their own women, smiling back at them with the reddest lips they had ever kissed.

Gene collected his emotions and cleared his throat "My God, big Joe, this is some kind of line up!" he said as he made his way down the line of beauties, Michael and James right behind him. Joe's prostitutes reached out to touch them, saying little words of encouragement and open invitations. Gene stopped in front of Susan.

"Well now, aren't you are a living doll! Young too!" Gene forced a smile, trying to hold in his anger, yet all the while, wanting to grabbed her into his arms and smother her with kisses.

A bleached blonde moved over next to him and ran a seductive hand down his strong arm, as her eyes feasted on his muscular body.

"Say handsome, why not pick me, a 'real' experienced woman who knows all the right moves! I'm sure I can offer you everything you need, better than this young thing!"

Gene smiled down into Susan's blue eyes, expecting her to fly off the handle. Instead, she held her true feeling in tack as she returned his smile and moved in closer to him.

"Don't believe everything you see or hear, mister! I may be young, but Roxanne can show you things you've never had before!" Susan ran her fingers slowly down his chest and stopped just above his growing erection.

Taking a heavy breath, Gene took Susan's arm. Never taking his eyes off hers, he spoke to the owner

"I will take this hot number, big Joe, to my house, my bed!"

"Wise choice Lucky, but you will have to take Tracy and Monica for your two friends. They come as a package deal." The heavy- set man motioned for Jackie and Ali "If they are willing to take them…" before Mr. Stallington could finish his statement, Michael grabbed Jackie and James pulled Ali over next to him. Scott laughed out at their quick reactions.

"My boys are easy to please." Gene caught the angry stares from Jackie and Ali and instantly read disapproval from his outspoken statement. With a twinkle in his eye, he reached over and pinched their cheek. "I must admit, the boys are doing as good as me, this time!' his eyes fell mischievously on Susan "If I didn't choose this little filly, I would grab both of them at the same time!"

This time, it was Michael and James who were frowning at the big man as Michael gave him a small push.

"Let's get going Lucky! I am about to pop out of my pants!" Michael started to pull Jackie toward the red door when big Joe stopped him.

"There is one more, small thing before you take these lovely ladies, gentlemen." The owner motioned to someone waiting just inside a side room. "These girls are the property of Phil Priencel. If you take these girls to your home, you must take Mr. Priencel as well. That is the deal, my friend."

Pogo walked in the room carrying four suitcases and Michael and James quickly turned their heads to hide their laughter at his appearance.

"Yes gentlemen, that is our deal." Pogo spoke with authority in a proper British accent.

Gene got in his face, anger dripping off each word that he spoke

"So, that's the deal, Pretzel? Then let me make this clear,

as long as you keep the hell out of my way when I am having fun with this sexy broad, then we will find you a room!"

"The name is Priencel, Mr. Walters, Phil Priencel, from New York!" Pogo started toward the door as Gene grabbed his arm.

"Listen, Phil Pretzel, from New York, get in my way and I will use you for an oil drill, understand?" Gene jerked one of the suitcases out of his arm then motioned for James and Michael to do the same. He took a firm hold on Susan's hand and pulled her to the car.

Chapter Fourteen

Reverend Gene Scott took his wife's arm and pulled her around to face him when he reached the car.

"Young lady, I will get you later!" he whispered "But for now, keep up the act! This car could have been bugged when we were inside!" he opened the passenger side and helped her in "Go ahead little darling, climb in and get ready for a ride!" Scott turned and walked over to James and spoke softly

"The car might be wired, so tell Ali to keep acting her part." Then he spoke out "Okay. Hot Shot, jump into the back seat with sexy Monica and try to control yourself until we reach the ranch, got it?"

"Sure thing, boss! I can wait if you have to." James patted Ali on her backend as she climbed in "Nice ass, Monica! Real cool!"

"Thanks Jimmy boy!" she laughed "Yours ain't so bad yourself!"

"Hot Shot, just get quiet!" Scott made his way over to where Pogo was getting into the big Lincoln Town car. He grabbed him by the collar and pulled him out, lifting him off the ground "Alright Pretzel, you little weasel, hand them over!"

"Hand what over, sir?" Pogo swallowed hard as he stared into his friend's angry eyes.

"The damn keys, Pretzel! Hand them over "Scott held out his other hand and lend in to the frighten young man and whispered "Both our cars could have been wired while we were inside that house of sin! They could be listening to every word we say, so keep acting!"

"Alright! Take the keys, Mr. Walters!" Pogo said loudly as he climbed in the back seat "And the name is Priencel!" he spoke with his British accent and Scott squinted his eyes at him.

"You don't say! Very well, Pretzel, whatever you say!" Gene faked a smile, then motioned for Michael and whispered the same warning to him before speaking out.

"Alright Bullseye, follow me to the ranch in this red monster and no hanky panky with Tracy, although she is one sexy broad!"

"Thanks, tall, dark, muscular, hot and sexy hunk!" Jackie winked at the handsome preacher "If you ever want to play swap, let me know!"

Michael frowned over at Jackie, then up to a smiling Scott.

"Alright, let's roll these babies! We've got the night ahead and I am ready to hit the sheets!" Gene climbed behind the wheel and started down the road. Susan rubbed her hand down the center of his legs. He closed his eyes and swallowed.

"Watch that, Foxy Roxie!" he glanced over at her "I'll take care of your sweet ass later!"

Susan laid her head back and smiled as she breathed in the night air. She had just felt her man growing hard from her touch and although he was mad at her, she knew it would not be for long.

The cars came to a stop just before reaching the front entrance. Gene got out and motioned for everyone to follow him. As they were climbing out, Scott said loudly

"We are home ladies! It's time to go inside and have a few drinks to get acquainted and then lots of fun and games!"

"Sounds good, Lucky, you, handsome devil!" Susan talked soft and sexy "I feel in the mood for a really good time, stud!"

The rest of the group joined in with many comments relating to fun and sex, then they moved quietly behind Scott to the dark rose garden.

"Alright, listen up!" Scott whispered in the dark moon light as he searched each face, his gaze lingering on Susan, her eyes shining in the moon's glow. He pulled his attention on the others "Except for George Martin, there are three town's people working here. Vera Simon, the cook, Maxine Fletcher, the housekeeper and Horus Hampton, the garner. Any or all of these people could be spies working for Joe and his big crime family. It's a pretty big operation, and despite their appearance, they can be dangerous!" Gene stared down at Susan "I never wanted any of you to be in danger but now you have made yourself part of the plan. I am giving you fair warning ladies" his blue eyes held Susan's "it is no time to be jealous, damn it!" Scott's eyes blazed "Like it or not, the boys and I have to get with those prostitutes sooner or later, to catch them in the act."

"What exactly do you mean by catching them in the act, unless you intend to do the 'act'!" Susan put her hands on her hips and stared up at Gene "Just explain that so I will understand just how far you are willing to go, Gene Scott!"

"Susan, damn it, woman! I am not going to have sex with anyone but you!" Scott noticed he had everyone's attention and they were listening closely, with big smiles spread across their faces. Michael caught Scott's disapproving look, so he quickly added, just as much to convince himself as he was Jackie.

"Girls, it is innocent, really. We get the girls drunk with wine laced with sleeping pills, they pass out, then we tell them how great they were. Right James?" Michael punched his friend's skinny arm.

"Right on, man! It's hip! The dumb broads fall for it every time! It's just one big act!" James reached for Ali's hand and she pulled away "Come on, sweetheart, we don't take out clothes off in front of them chicks!"

"Oh sure!" Ali turned and stared up angrily at Gene Scott "You might not take your clothes off, but I know you hug them and kiss them! These women are not stupid as you think! They are the ones that slip drugs into your drinks to get you hooked!"

"What do you girls take us for, a bunch of push overs?"

Scott grabbed Pogo, who had been taking in the little argument "You had better have a little talk with your jealous whores here before I spank their sweet ass!"

"I am sure I can get them to calm down Scott, but for now, that staff of spies are probably wondering where we are." Pogo forced a smile at the angry face "Scott?"

"Alright Pretzel, you are right! We must not keep the spies suspicious as to our where about!" Gene took Susan by the arm and pulled her to the front door. "Little Foxy Roxie, you and I are going through that front door and we are going to be in a happy fun-loving way! Got that, sweetheart?"

"By all means! Let's go, Lucky! I can act just as good as you!" Susan pushed the door open and threw her arms around Scott's neck, laughing. "Oh Lucky, you hot talking man! I am ready to show you a good time in the sack!" she smiled up at a bewildered Martin as though she were intoxicated. He blinked and swallowed as he recognized Scott's wife. Susan reached over and patted Martin's cheek.

"Well, hello there handsome! Where have you been hiding?" She heard Michael and James sneaker as Gene pulled her back over in his arms.

"I had better get this little sweet ass up to bed before she gets away!" Gene lifted Susan into his strong arms and started up the steps.

"Oh Mr. Clint, sir?" Vera Simon stood smiling from the bottom step "I've laid out some wonderful refreshments for you and your guest." She gazed aggravated at Martin "I finally convinced Mr. Haywood to help with the wine and drinks sir."

Scott frowned down at the fake butler "Haywood, that is one of your jobs! Now see to it that our guest is served!"

"Very good, sir." George Martin lifted his nose into the air and started pouring drinks.

"What about you sir and the little woman?" the cook smiled broadly watching her gallant boss holding tight to his woman. "Refreshments?"

Gene looked down into Susan's eyes, but this time her eyes were not mocking or pretending. They were filled with love and passion for the man she loved. Without taking his eyes off the girl who held his heart, he called down.

"Vera, darling, I have all the refreshments I need right here." Gene made his way to his bedroom and shut the door with his foot. He bent down until his lips melted over hers. Setting her down gently, he walked over to his dresser to retrieve a tissue to wipe away the red lipstick from his lips, then repeated taking off Susan's lipstick. Gene smiled down lovingly and pulled his wife in his arms.

"Now, that's my girl!" he easily lifted Susan's trim body back into his muscular arms and carried her to the extra- large king size bed where he laid her down. Gene Scott stretched his tall frame next to her and let his hand slide inside her low- cut blouse, cupping his strong hand gently around her young breast. Feeling her nipple grow hard under his touch, his passion for her swelled. Taking a firm hold on the red blouse, he pulled it over her head, then he removed the hairpins from her up-sweep twist and let her long black hair fall over her shoulders. Pulling her against him, Gene began kissing her neck.

Susan closed her eyes as she took a deep breath of relief. Gene was not mad at her and he needed her as much as she needed him. She could feel his erection pressing up against her as she reached over and removed his black silk shirt. Susan whispered softly in his ear

"Nice shirt, Mr. Scott."

Gene laughed softly as he undone her red push up bra and took around each breast "Nice breast, Mrs. Scott." He whispered.

"You like them? They belong to my husband." She ran her hands down his back.

"You're damn right!" Gene smiled mischievously as his mouth lowered down over the harden nipple.

"Gene Scott!" Susan pulled at his zipper "If you don't start making love to me pretty soon, I'm going to explode!"

Gene yanked off his pants and tossed his boxers on the floor next to them. He pulled Susan's short skirt and red underwear off, then filled her with uncontrollable passion until they reached their fireworks, exploding in an array of sparks and colors.

Gene and Susan lay exhausted, wrapped in one another's arms. Gene slowly ran his fingers through her tossed hair.

"God, I love you Susan. I should be mad as hell that you came, but damn, I'm glad you did!"

Chapter Fifteen

"Susan! Susan?" She felt a soft hand shaking her shoulder as she struggled to open her eyes. "Wake up Susan, it's Jackie. You need to come with us to our rooms."

Susan looked up and saw Jackie holding a robe. She turned and looked at her husband, who was sleeping soundly, then back up at Jackie, confused.

"What? I don't understand, our rooms? This is my room."

"No Susan, this is Clint Walters' room. If the staff catch you here coming out with Scott, they might get suspicious." Jackie pulled her up out of the king size bed and put the robe around her naked body. "Where are your clothes?"

"They…I think Gene threw them on the floor, his side." Susan tried to focus her eyes and wake up.

Jackie laughed softly as she separated Susan's clothes from her husband's, then she smiled down at the sleeping hunk.

"My, he must have yanked them off you both. Couldn't wait, Scott?"

"As if you or Michael could!" Susan took her clothes and started to follow her friend when Gene reach out and took her arm.

"Where do you think you're going, Susan?"

"To my room 'Lucky', mustn't let the help gossip." Susan bent down and kissed him "Sleep tight, darling."

"You too, Foxy Roxie." Gene winked at her and rolled over "Shut the door behind you. I don't want Vera sneaking in."

"Very funny Scott!" Jackie whispered as she pulled Susan out the door. They could see Ali standing at the end of the hall, looking from side to side. When she spotted the two outside Scott's room, she made her way quickly to them.

"It's about time you two came out! I was beginning to think you decided to crawl into bed with them!"

"I admit, it was tempting." Jackie laughed at Susan's eyebrow going up "Just kidding, Roxanne." At the end of the hall, she opened a door and walked inside to a big, luxurious room, decorated very feminine. There were three queen size beds tucked separately apart, within a cozy cove. "Isn't this a lovely bedroom Susan? We've got one large bathroom and three, walk- in closets."

"Michael and James filled us in on the bedroom situation." Ali crawl into one of the beds "Then sweet Mr. Martin showed us to our room after a few 'They know not what they do' under his breath."

Jackie stretched her arms and laughed "Mike told the good reverend, if he wanted to live to see another day, he had better stop preaching and stick to being a heathen butler or Scott would cut his life short."

"George Martin can get on one's nerves." Susan undone the third bed and climbed under the covers "I just hope he doesn't give us away." She turned the light off and whispered, "I cannot believe Gene is right down the hall and I'm in here!"

"Go to sleep, Roxanne." Jackie mumbled sleepily as she yawned "Big Clint Walters paid for a week of loving. He will get his money's worth again tomorrow!"

When Susan and her friends got up, they dressed in tight jeans and light low-cut sweaters. After strapping on extra high heels and light make-up, they made their way downstairs. The big entry hall was quiet as Susan whispered

"Where is everyone this morning? I know I would hear Gene if he were up."

"Who knows, Roxanne!" Ali nudged Susan's arm playfully "Lucky is probably in the breakfast room having a hardy breakfast with his two side- kicks. If his mouth is full, you can't hear his strong voice booming out." She pushed open the swinging door to the breakfast room and walked in to find Pogo sitting quietly, eating alone.

"Good morning ladies. Come and join me in breakfast. It's very good." Pogo stood like a gentleman and pulled a chair out for each girl. "I trust you ladies slept well having done your find work last night with the gentlemen." He motioned toward the kitchen door to let them know someone could be listening to their conversation.

"We had a very restful night, Phil darling. Those gents really know their moves and I can honestly say, they were amazed at ours." Jackie looked at the kitchen door as she spoke in a normal voice "What, does one have to do to get breakfast around here?"

Vera Simon came quickly through the big kitchen door carrying a tray filled with three plates of bacon and eggs.

"Good morning ladies. Mr. Clint told me to be sure you had a good breakfast." The cook looked at the beautiful group of strangers, then she spotted the girl the handsome preacher had carried up the stairs the previous night "Are you Roxanne?"

"I'm Roxanne, yes." Susan smiled warmly "Did Lucky say something about me?"

"As a matter of fact, child, Mr. Clint was all smiles this morning and I do not think it was because of that hardy breakfast I sat in front of him." Vera winked at Susan "Mr. Clint told me that Roxanne was extra good last night and make sure she got everything she wanted." The cook placed a plate in front of each girl and a rose at Susan's, as she chuckled with joy "I can see Mr. Clint likes 'em young."

"My girls always seem to please, Mrs. Simon." Pogo poured coffee for everyone "Men just can't get enough."

"Yes, which brings me to my next question. Everyone knows big Joe's top girls usually get the best jobs." Vera looked puzzle "How come he let your girls get these clients?"

"How do you know so much about Joe's girls, Mrs.

Simon?" Jackie casually took a sip of the hot coffee "Have you worked at Joe's Beauties before?"

"Good Lord! No child!" Vera laughed loudly "This is a small town, my dear. Everyone living in Greystone know Joe's girls. They go about the streets shopping and eating out, like everyone else. The locals are accustomed to them being around and think nothing of it. Those ladies don't just sit behind those fancy doors waiting for a rich client to come in for business."

"Lucky tells me you have several sons, Vera. Please don't think me rude, but have they given Joe any business?" Susan took a bite of her toast.

"Well, they wouldn't be telling their mama if they did." She chuckled "But seeing to how they are healthy boys and all, I would not doubt it none."

"That will be all, Mrs. Simon. We would not want to keep you from your duties." Pogo stood and patted his full stomach "Your breakfast was excellent."

"Yes, it was Vera, thank you." Susan got up and followed Pogo to the door "You can tell Mr. Walters I said thank you."

"I will madam. I'm glad you enjoyed it.' After putting the empty plates back on the tray, she slipped back in the kitchen.

Pogo led the three girls to the rose garden. The cool morning air felt refreshing as it blew off the good smelling roses. Susan shielded her eyes as she scanned her surroundings. The Texas plane lay stretched out in front of her.

"Just where the devil is Lucky? It is too early in the day to be looking for another hooker!' she gritted her teeth at the thought.

"I don't think he would go back this soon Roxanne." Jackie took Susan's hand "Remember what he said about getting jealous."

"I am not jealous! I just don't want Joe to think Clint Walters is already tired of me!" she could sense by her companions faces that they were not alone. Susan turned quickly and stared into Gene's chest.

"Now, Foxy Roxie, do you think old Clint is ever going to

get tired of you, you, sexy little siren!" he grabbed Susan and kissed her.

Susan's face turned red as she pulled at her tight sweater "Out for a ride this morning, Lucky?"

"I was." He smiled wickedly "But it wasn't as good as the ride I had last night!"

Susan started to hit Gene when she noticed the ground's keeper looking. "You sir, are a big tease." She forced a laugh "If you think last night was good, just wait until tonight, stud! The best is yet to come."

"I say, bring it on, baby doll!" Gene's eyes lit up with mischief "Old Lucky just keeps getting luckier!" Gene threw his hand up to Horus Hampton "Morning Horus! You got everything looking real pretty out here! Do you want me to fetch you a little filly for tonight? You've earned it"

"No thank you, sir." The garner turned quickly and started hoeing out a few weeds from around the roses.

Scott nodded his head toward the garner and whispered, "Mr. Hampton makes it look like he is busy working but you can easily tell he is listening to every word we say." Scott pretended to be checking out the roses as he raised his voice loud enough for the ease dropper to hear "Well ladies, there is a lot to do around here during the daytime. The night time…" Gene laughed lazily "well, the nights belong to me and the boys!" he winked at Susan as he continued "Look, you may choose horseback riding, tennis, even golf, but you ladies look more like the pool type and I have got a very big one on the south side of the ranch house." Gene reached over and caressed Susan's face "I just bet some of you love a big swimming pool."

"That really sounds wonderful Lucky." She returned his previous wink "Girls, I guess we will have to skinny dip since we didn't bring swimsuits."

"I don't mind." Ali laughed softly at the men's dropped jaws "I'm really used to taking off my clothes. I got over being shy years ago."

"Same here!" Jackie patted Scott's arm "There is nothing I like better than swimming in the nude. It's such a warm experience."

"Girl, girls?" Gene smiled shaky "You're killing me here. The boy and I would not get any work done around here if you three lovely ladies were flashing your wares."

"Then, what do you suggest we do Lucky? Wearing your swim trunks pulled up with a belt?" Susan and the others laughed at the thought.

"It just so happens I'm going into town on some business." Gene smiled at Susan's angry glare "I think you ladies might just accompany me and my boys and go shopping for new swimsuits, my treat! I have set up a tab in the finer shops lining Greystone streets."

"Are these shops suitable for ladies like us?" Jackie took Scott's arm "Lucky, the three of us prefer hot sexy clothing, darling."

Gene Scott laughed out "Tracy, are there any other kind of shops in Greystone? This town is crawling with prostitutes. I am sure they all cater to please their best customers. The homely women have to shop at the Sears in the next town."

"Then that sounds perfect! What are we waiting for?" Ali started to move when Scott took her arm and looked over the girl's outfits and high shoes.

"May I make a suggestion, ladies?"

"Shoot Lucky!" Susan smiled up into his blue eyes.

"A change of wardrobe that is better for shopping, not to mention those extra high heels need to be replaced by comfortable walking shoes." Gene noticed Jackie and Ali narrowing their eyes at him "Ladies, those very sexy heels may be find for your line of work or…even church services…"

All three girls got choked from his unexpected remark and Scott and Pogo slapped their backs until they could breathe normally.

"Ladies, I really think you would be a lot happier in good

walking shoes." Gene smiled at their frowning faces "The streets are hard concrete and there are probably uneven places to turn your ankle or break a heel off. But do what suits you. I was once in Africa and these three broads refused to listen to me about wearing long pants in the jungle, instead of their cute little shorts. As I recall, they were nearly eaten up by mosquitos!" he rolled his eyes up as he shook his head "Do as you please, but if I were you…"

"Give us ten minutes!" Jackie turned toward the big ranch house, calling back "On second thought, make that twenty!" she raced off, Ali right behind her. Susan reached up and pinched her husband's cheek lightly.

"You are so wise, Lucky, thank you for looking after us." Susan blew him a kiss and hurried off to catch her friends.

Gene checked his watch "Well, Pretzel, now we wait!' Scott patted his young friend's shoulder as he sat down on a garden bench to wait.

"Things are really looking up around here! Going shopping!" Ali walked inside their room and suddenly noticed Maxine Fletcher watching them from the bathroom mirror, while she cleaned it off. Ali made a face toward the bathroom then continued, talking in character. "Not only have we got great paying jobs, making three hot sexy men happy, we have got shopping and activities to keep us busy during the day."

"Yes, it's almost like being married!" Susan laughed, joined by her friends "There's only one difference, when we grow tired of them, we just pack up and leave."

"If they don't get tired of you first, dear." Maxine Fletcher walked from the bathroom with her bucket of cleaning supplies. "I never meant to ease drop, but in your line of work, men grow tired of you sooner or later and want someone younger and prettier."

"You sound as though you know a lot about a hooker's life, Miss Fletcher." Jackie laced up her shoes "I'm curious, were you ever a prostitute?"

"Just between you and me, let's say at one time I was at the top of the list." Her mind seemed to float back to another time. "I was once a beautiful girl, then too many men, just faces and bodies now. It changed when I became hooked..." she stopped short.

"Hooked on what, Maxine?" Susan walked over and put her hand on the woman's trembling shoulders "May I call you Maxine?"

"Of course, you may, dear." She looked into Susan's sincere eyes "I have said enough. I am a foolish old woman! Go shopping and enjoy your day. Mr. Clint will get mad if you are late coming down." Maxine picked up her bucket and walked quickly from their room.

"Well, whatever it was, I don't believe Miss Fletcher will bring that subject up again." Jackie frowned as she followed Susan and Ali down the hall to the stairs. "Hooked on what?"

Chapter Sixteen

Gene paced back and forth waiting for the girls. He watched Michael and James making their way cross the large brick courtyard toward him.

"Already to go…" Michael spotted the garner watching "Lucky? I will bring the Mercedes around."

"Yeh, sure, and you boys can bring the red Town Car around too. The girls are coming along to go shopping." Scott stuck some gum in his mouth as he waved his two friends off toward the garage.

"Oh brother!" James mumbled as he followed Michael to get the cars "Those women and their shopping!" his eyes fell on the two big cars "Hey Dave, let me drive the Mercedes."

"Are you kidding, Jim? You are more a Lincoln man!" Michael laughed at his friend's fallen expression as he climbed behind the wheel of the expensive automobile. James narrowed his eyes in discuss as he climbed in the red Lincoln Town Car.

As Scott stood waiting, his attention was drawn to Horus Hampton trimming the big variety of shrubs in the Botanical garden. Gene's eyebrow shot up as the gardener turned his attention to a large flowing bush whose golden flowered branches cascaded down to the ground. He raised his clippers to begin pruning when Gene's voice called out loudly, "Hey Horus, stop my good man right where you are!" with quick footsteps the tall preacher stood over the frightened man "What the hell do you think you're doing?"

"Shaping this untidy shrub sir." The garner's hand trembled.

"Relax Horus!" Gene patted the man's thin back "No harm done. This little Yellow Bell bush is supposed to grow free and flowing, not cut into a damn square shrub, understand?"

"Sure thing, Mr. Clint. I only thought…" he swallowed.

"The morning sun is starting to heat things up out here, my good man. Just give the garden a rest and if you will, please get the pool ready. My guest will want to use it when we return from town." Gene's eyes fell on Susan leading Jackie and Ali his way. "Now scoot! Then have a drink and take the rest of the day off!" Scott winked at the smiling man then made his way to Susan.

"I must say you ladies looked much more comfortable." He laughed "Besides, there's no need for you to advertise your wares, you already belong to us men who bought that privilege."

Susan deliberately stepped heavily on her husband's toe. Gene pulled her tight into his arms smiling as Michael drove the Mercedes to a stop next to the big man. Opening the back door, Gene lifted Susan's face with his hand.

"Foxy Roxie, you ride in the back with me. Hot Hips, up front with lucky Dave."

"My treat!" Jackie laughed and climbed in close to Michael. Smiling up into his blue eyes, she laid her hand on his upper leg. "Drive slow, sweetheart."

Gene draped his arm around the woman he loved and patted the back of Michael's head lightly.

"Roll these wheels, Bullseye!" Gene waved his spare hand over his head at the trailing Lincoln to follow. James climbed over in the back seat, pulling Ali over with him, and took her in his arms.

"Pretzel, you drive. I'm more of a Mercedes man!"

Pogo mumbled to himself as he put the car into gear "Shit, I am the forth man 'out'! Everyone has a woman except me! I really want some loving!"

"Hey Phil, did you say something up there?" James continued to caress Ali.

"No, nothing that would interest you, Hot Shot!" Pogo glanced up in the rearview mirror at the love birds necking, lost in each other. "Just thinking out loud, lover boy!"

In the lead car, Gene Scott lifted Susan's face up and kissed her with tenderness, then he whispered in her ear

"I love you, Susan Scott."

Susan's face radiated in a beautiful smile as she threw her legs over his lap and looped her arms around his strong neck in a hug. She pulled his head down to kiss him as she spoke softly

"I love you too, Gene Scott." They continued kissing all the way to Greystone city limits.

"Alright you two love birds!" Michael patted the back of his seat to get their attention "We are about to drive into sin city. You'd better come up for air."

Gene ran his fingers through his hair to straighten out his curls. Turning around to check on the car following them, he noticed Ali was wiping her lipstick off James with a tissue. Scott stretched his strong arms and smiled broadly.

"Damn, it's good to be alive!"

Michael nodded his head in agreement as he pulled the car over in front of a row of dress shops. Gene patted Susan's knee.

"O.K. sweetheart, hop out and get to shopping. We should be back in about one hour."

"One hour?" Jackie forced a smile at Scott "Alright. That should be enough time for three, maybe four shops." She waved over her head at the four men watching, and hurried the other girls along. In her lovely British accent, she called back to the four watching "Wait for us dolls, if you get back first!" Jackie disappeared behind Ali and Susan as they went inside the Hot & Sexy Lady's Apparels.

"Now that we have our women occupied, we can pay a visit to Joe's Beauties." Gene climbed into the front seat while James took his place in the back. Pogo started to get in behind with James when Scott waved him out. "You stay here with the Town Car, Pretzel. We will be right back." Gene turned to his driver "Alright Dave, let's roll!"

"Take your time, fellows!" Pogo mumbled to himself as he watched the black Mercedes drive away "When those three ladies go shopping, Lord, that one hour can easily turn into two, maybe three. I for one do not want to be standing here that long with an angry Scott!"

Reverend Scott stared at the big red door for a moment before ringing the bell. He whispered to his two companions "Listen fellows, let me do the talking."

"That suits me, don't worry." Michael frowned up at the tall man "Please tell me you are not ready for a new model?"

"Shit no!" Scott mumbled "Susan would kill me if I even suggested coming back so quick. It would make her appear she was not good enough for me."

"Then, what are we doing here so soon?" James listened to the sound of footsteps approaching from the big house.

"Not to change our women, so relax and just stay quiet, damn it!" Scott watched the red door open and saw Joe himself smiling up at him.

"Lucky, my man, back so soon for another woman?"

"Naw, it is defiantly not for another woman Big Joe!" Scott laughed out "The three of us are very pleased with our choice!"

"Then, if it's not for another woman, my friend, tell me what it is you want from me?" The robust owner waved for a maid to bring drinks in.

"My sources tell me you might know someone who...well, sales the good stuff." Gene patted the well dress man on his back as he took a drink off the round tray and thanks the flirty maid.

"The good stuff, I see." Joe took a big gulp of the whisky as he let the big man's words sink in "Lucky, my friend, I hardly know you. Let us take this a little slower." The owner of the fancy whore house gave Scott a genial smile as he studied for the right words to say for such a bold request. "I cannot rush into such matters and besides, you or your boys have not tasted the lips of my beautiful ladies yet."

"I have a lot of money, Joe; I know how this works. Cash for a stash, so they say." Scott walked around, pretending to be interest in the art on the walls as he remained cool "What do you say my friend?"

"Very well, Lucky, I will make a deal with you. You choose one of my girls and give me your full business, then I shall see if I can be of some service to you. Trust me Lucky, your odds will get a whole lot better!" Joe Stallington lit a cigar and offered one to Scott, who took it and put it inside his shirt pocket.

"Thanks Joe, I will have this later." Gene smiled broadly "Very well, Joe, I understand your being careful, me new to these parts and all. At the moment, I have plenty of the good stuff on hand, but if I remain in the area, I shall have to find a new supplier."

"Yes, of course Lucky, my friend. I am sure we can work something out." Big Joe walked the three visitors to the door "And you are sure the young little lady is working out for you?"

"Very much Joe! Like you said, she's young plus she is very exciting, not to mention one hell of a lover in bed." Gene started through the door when he heard the owner laughed mischievously.

"I was sure she must be a good lover. I even considered keeping her for my own personal lover!" he winked at the serious face Scott. "Perhaps when you are finished with her, I will take her to my bed."

Gene Scott felt his blood began to boil as he balled his fist up tightly and narrowed his eyes at the smiling man. He felt the vein in his neck grow tense as he forced out his words as normal as possible.

"Well Joe, I do not intend to give her up any time soon so stop dreaming!" Scott turned and walked quickly from the house, mumbling to himself. When they reached the car, James let out his breath in relief.

"Shit Scott, I thought you were going to cream that fat creep!" he opened the car door for the angry preacher.

"Just get this damn car out of here before I go back in there and plaster his sorry ass to the wall!" Gene glared out the car window.

"What kind of jerk is that anyway?" Michael drove the big car quickly out of the shady driveway "He has a wife, for God's sake!"

"My good friend Mike, men like that do not give a damn about their wedding vows! People's feelings mean absolutely nothing to that bastard!" Gene angrily hit the back of the car seat "He is just a stinking drug pusher and a whore salesman! Joe Stallington is the stinking scum of the earth!"

"Shit! And we are in 'hot water'!" James stared back at Scott "If this car is bugged, we have been found out!"

"Damn!" Scott yelled "Did you fellows check it out like I ask?"

"We really gave it a going over this morning and we couldn't find anything." Michael gave him a reassuring smile in the rearview mirror "We know all the good hiding places in an automobile and we can always spot a listening device hidden. We haven't failed yet Scott. Trust me, it's clean. James is just being a little mellow dramatic."

"Well, sure, Mikes right man! I just lost my cool for a moment. You can rest with ease. This baby is as clean as a nun!" James tried to laugh it off.

"What about just now, when we were inside? Someone could have slipped a device in after I ask about buying drugs?" Scott had to be reassured the crooks hadn't heard them.

"You can relax Scott, we thought of that too." Michael smiled over at his skinny friend "James installed a clever device that goes off loudly if someone so much as touches the car and it rings out until I put the key in the lock."

James laughed "The key is the only entry without setting off my sure -fire alarm system! Sorry I lost my cool earlier Scott. We're safe."

"Good, we getting close to finding something out." Gene climbed out when Michael stopped the car in front of the shops. After checking his watch, Gene looked up the street for any sign of the girls. They had been gone for one hour and thirty minutes since going to the house of prostitution. Gene motioned for Pogo, who had been busy watching the pretty women coming and going. He walked lazily to where the three men were waiting.

"Pogo, have you seen the girls yet?"

Pogo grew anxious, worried that the wired cars would pick up their conversation, so he placed his finger over his lips before he answered his friend.

"No, Mr. Walters. I never expected they would be finished with their shopping in one hour."

"Relax Pogo, we're safe, the cars are not bugged." Michael laughed "I knew Jackie would take at least two hours."

"Two hours? More like three, if we're lucky." James started to lend back on the Mercedes when Scott pulled him over to him. "Hey man, I'm not responsible for my chick!"

Gene chuckled and pulled a twenty- dollar bill from his wallet and placed it in his hip friend's hand.

"Cool it James!" Scott winked "I just want you to take this money inside that good smelling candy shop across the street and buy us a big bag of candy."

"Sure thing, daddy-o. What kind, chocolate?" James stared to make his way lazily across the quiet street.

"Is there any other kind?" Scott was still feeling the effects from the vile man's comments about Susan when he frowned at the long legs of James, making his way slowly across the street. When he reached the other side, James turned and chugged his thin shoulders, waiting for orders.

"Yes James, chocolate! Try to save some for the rest of

us!" Scott lend up against the big Mercedes between Michael and Pogo to wait.

Moments later, Michael raised up slightly and whispered as he poked Gene's strong arm "Check out those three prostitutes walking toward us."

Reverend Scott chuckled as they twisted their way to them. He spoke softly to his companions. "Skirts up to their ass, tops down to their navel and heels as high as a ten- foot ladder."

Michael and Pogo laughed, then Michael lend over to whisper "And enough make-up to paint a ship!"

Smiling seductively, the three flirty prostitutes stopped in front of the three handsome men. The bleached blonde that had made passes at him on the night he left with Susan, reached over and rubbed her soft hand up Gene's arm.

"Well now, if it isn't Clint Walters! My, my, don't you look handsome, standing there, relaxing against your car."

"Are you fellows waiting for us, doll?" a bright red-head popped her chewing gum as she checked the men over.

"Actually ladies, we are waiting for three very sexy ladies of our own." Gene Scott forced a smile.

"Tell me hunk, do you mean those three girls that came barging into our business?" the blonde moved closer to the tall preacher and caressed his cheek "My dear Mr. Walters, I can show you a lot more fun than that young child you chose with no experience."

Michael punched Gene's arm and nodded his head toward Susan, who had spotted the hookers and she was making her way swiftly their way.

"Ladies, for your own good, I think you had better move on!" Scott had a twinkle in his eyes "I do not think you want to tangle with Miss Roxanne."

"Lucky darling…: she patted her false eyelashes "I hope you don't mine my calling you Lucky, but trust me, darling, I am not afraid of a child."

"Just who the hell are you calling a child?" Susan had

reached them and slung her packages in Gene's hands and turned to face the woman flirting with her husband. "I'll have you know, I am older than I look, you bimbo!"

Gene quickly handed the packages to Pogo so his hands would be free.

"Look sweetie, you are young enough to be Lucky's daughter!" the blonde gave Susan a faux smile "What could you possibly know about pleasing a real man?"

"Look 'sweetie', it is because I am young Lucky picked me, you bitch! I'm fresh, unused, I'm extremely talented in sex, and I will outlast your sorry ass any day, sister!"

"Well, I never!" the hooker glared in Susan's angry eyes for a moment, then turned her attention on the smiling preacher "Look handsome, when you get tired of this child, I'll be waiting! Willing! Hot!"

"Beside doll, what we got to offer you is so much more than sex!" the redheaded hooker winked at her friends as they turned and twisted on down the street laughing.

Susan started to follow them in a rage, when her husband lifted her off the ground. She squirmed around in his embrace, trying to free herself.

"Put me down! I am going to pull that blonde hair out by its dark roots! The man chaser!"

"Susan, calm down darling." Scott laughed out "I think those 'ladies' know how you feel about them."

"What is going on down here?" Jackie stormed up carrying an armload of packages "Susan, I hope you gave those damn whores what they had coming!"

"Oh, she did, hon, just a red- hot spitfire." Michael joined Scott in laughter.

"Shit, why wasn't I here? I would have knocked all three on their sorry asses!" Ali stared down the street at the prostitutes who kept glancing back at the men.

Gene had noticed James walking up behind the girls, listening intensely at their angry words. The more he listened, the faster his hand dived into the bag of candy and gram in his mouth, one piece after another. Gene Scott reached over and grabbed the bag out of his hand, startling him.

"James, give me that bag of candy before you eat it all! You looked like Weber!"

James smiled sheepishly as he wiped the melted chocolate off his lips and watched Scott pass the candy around to the group. Gene held the bag up in front of Pogo as he placed one of the creamy confections in his mouth and gave his friend an approving wink.

"Have a piece pal, it is really good!"

"No thank you Scott. I am watching my weight." Pogo could smell the fresh aroma of chocolate under his nose as he stared at the white bag.

"Come on Pogo, I know you want some." Taking a piece out, Gene handed it to Susan, then turned back to his friend who was staring at the bag, licking his lips. "You know you want some."

Pogo's face grew crimson, thinking his friend was referring to his statement he had made about wanting a woman in the car coming to town. "How…how could you possibly know what I said about wanting some? You were not even in the car." He could tell suddenly by Gene's confused expression that he had no idea what his young friend was talking about. Pogo forced a shaky laugh as he reached inside the bag and pulled a piece of chocolate out. "I was just telling myself in the car coming to town, I could really go for a piece of chocolate candy." He quickly stuck the candy in his mouth and let it melt. "Say, that is good! I think I will have another piece!"

"Your'e watching your weight, remember Pogo?" Scott laughed as he closed the bag and motioned for the group to get into the cars, ignoring Pogo's disappointment. "Let's get out of this sin city before we all start cursing!" he pushed the candy bag in Pogo's hand and chuckled.

Chapter Seventeen

The girls walked out to the large pool. The day had grown hot and the sparkling water looked refreshing and inviting. Susan pulled off her cover revealing a yellow bikini.

"Last one in is a loser!" Susan ran to the water, Jackie and Ali close behind her. Smiling, all three jumped in at the same time getting an instant shock from the frigid water.

"GOOD LORD!" Jackie let out a scream "This feels like ice water!"

Ali looked around her in the water and shivered "Did some jerk put ice blocks in here?" she quickly made her way to the ladder, climbed out and retrieved her big towel to wrap around her. Finally feeling some warmer from her towel and the overhead sun, Ali looked out in the pool to see Susan swimming. "Susan, how on earth can you stand that ice water?"

Susan swam to the far end and looked over to find her two companions resting on lounge chairs.

"Hey girls, it's not so bad when you get used to it. It feels quite pleasant when you stay in for a while."

"I for one choose lying here soaking up the tanning rays." Jackie pulled out her suntan lotion "My tan could use a refresher."

"Mine too!" Susan climbed out and dried herself off "At lease it doesn't feel so hot out here after that cool swim." She caught motion from the huge sliding glass doors "We're getting company! Here come the guys!"

Gene, Michael and James made their way over, smiling and admiring the three bathing beauties stretched out on towels.

"Hello ladies, looking good! How's the water?" Gene stretched his long muscular arms to warm up for swimming.

"The water?" Jackie smiled at her bathing companions "The water is very refreshing, fellows, quite wonderful." She sat up for a better view of the pool "I would honestly say, it really cools you down quickly! Wouldn't you girls?"

"Most certainly! One dip in that lovely pool helps relieve you from the extra hot temperature out here, in the big Texas sun!" Ali tried not to laugh.

"It certainly does the trick!" Susan winked at Gene "It makes you feel cool as a cucumber."

"Great! I'm about to burn up out here." Gene climbed up the diving board and yelled to the empty pool below him "Look out below!" his big frame made a splash in the frigid water as he went to the bottom and sprang quickly back to the service. "What the shit! This is ice water!"

Michael and James bent over laughing as they watched their big friend shivering.

"Ah, come on old man! You've got to be young to take pool water when you first jump in!" Michael climbed up the ladder, still laughing.

"Then jump in, you, tough young jerk, and show me how the young outdo us older people!" Gene narrowed his eyes at Michael as he did a couple jumps before taking a somersault off the board into the cold water.

"HOLY COW! This is a damn iceberg!" Michael yelled as Scott chuckled loudly.

"What's the matter fellows, too cold?" Ali bent over laughing at the two men shaking in the water. "Go ahead James, get in and give it try. Show those funny men how it done!"

"I think I'll just sit down here and put my feet in the water." Sitting down on the edge of the pool, James slowly put his feet in the cold water. He turned and smiled at the girls "You know, get in slowly, a little bit at a time to get used to it."

"James, it's a whole lot easier to jump in all at once." Ali slipped up behind him and gave him a push into the refrigerated water. The other girls joined her in laughing.

"Shit Ali!" James reached up and grabbed her foot, pulling her into the cold water with him. All three fellows started laughing as she slung her arms around, trying to hit him, while spitting out pool water. "Now, whose laughing, babe?"

"James Tabor!" her voice shook "I orda kill you!"

Gene laughed and went under for a moment and sprung back up in front of the lounge chairs.

"Hey girls, it's not bad when you've been in here for a while." Gene smiled at his wife "Sweetheart, come in and join me!"

"I think I'm fine right here." Susan returned his smile "I really need to work on my fading tan."

"Susan, you wouldn't be a chicken, would you?" Gene teased "Where is that girl who grew up with a swimming pool at every house?"

Susan's eyes narrowed as she got up and climbed up the diving board "I will show you mister! I am no chicken!" she made a perfect dive and swam out to him "Now eat your words, Scott!"

"I'd much rather kiss you woman!' Gene pulled Susan into his strong arms as his lips parted over hers in a passionate kiss. "Besides, it got you out here with me!"

Ali smiled over at the romantic couple, completely loss in each- other's arms.

"Now James, do you see, that is how to treat a woman!"

"Like this?" James pulled Ali back and smothered her with a long kiss. She smiled up into his eyes.

"Exactly like that! Do it again, stud!"

"My pleasure, you, sexy chick!"

Gene looked up and smiled at James and Ali, then his attention was drawn to Michael, sitting next to Jackie. Swimming to the side of the pool, Scott climbed out and extended his hands to pull Susan up out of the water.

"We might as well get out and have a snack, I'm starving!" Scott reached up and pulled a rope connected to a bell inside the mansion, alerting Martin that lunch was to be served. Vera Simon and Horus Hampton made their way out the sliding doors next to the pool area pushing two carts. One with small sandwiches and fruit, the other with beer and wine. The cheerful cook smiled broadly at her boss.

"Here are the snacks you ask for Mr. Clint. I hope you enjoy the assortment of finger sandwiches I made."

"Mrs. Simon, they look good enough to eat!" Gene teased as she giggled like a schoolgirl. "As always, you have outdone yourself! You are a doll!" he winked at her round happy face then looked over at the garner "I see you are doing Heywood's job, Horus."

"Mr. Heywood will be out shortly to serve the drinks Mr. Walters." Horus said softly "I offered to bring them out when he got a telephone call, sir." The garner looked over the sun bathers and noticed they had all used the pool. "I take it the pool had cooled down, sir?"

"You might use the word cool, Horus. I prefer the word cold!" Gene noticed the garner turned pale "You didn't, by any chance, add something to the water to make it frigid, did you?"

"I might have got carried away sir." Horus Hampton looked apologetic at the group in front of him "The sun had made the water rather warm, so I called in for ice blocks and had the truck to dump the full load in the large pool. I never dreamed it would make it freezing, sir."

"No harm done Horus, it was a shock at first, but felt very refreshing once you got used to it." Gene patted his shoulder "Just skip the ice next time." He noticed the cook was still standing there listening "Vera, was there something else on your mine before you return to your kitchen?"

"I just wanted to say thank you sir." She laughed hardy "Mr. Heywood should be out here soon, although it took a lot of persuading. I just do not understand that man's behavior, sir. You would think I was asking him to commit a sin." Vera shook her head and went back inside, Mr. Hampton dragging behind her.

"I swear, that George Martin is a pain in my ass!" Gene frowned down at the heavy minister when he joined them, and rolled up his sleeves. "Reverend Martin, is fixing a few drinks too much for you to handle or do I need to kick your sorry ass home?"

"Actually, no sir, no trouble at all." Martin smiled sheepishly "After sampling a little of the fruit of the vine, I find it very pleasing to the taste. I really did not know what I was missing." He lifted up an empty glass and smiled down at the three seated women "Alright ladies, will it be white or red?"

"Oh God, what habit will brother George pick up next?" Pogo had overheard George's revelation just as he joined the group and walked between James and Michael to whisper. Gene Scott was standing close enough to hear Pogo's comments as he continued "Maybe the two of us can go into town and pick up a couple of prostitutes!'

James and Michael laughed as they tried to picture the unlikely pair with those whores and grabbed a couple of cold beer from the cart. Gene walked up next to his young friend and slapped him on the back as he dismissed George Martin, having him leave the cart behind. He rubbed Pogo playfully on the head, while laughing.

"Better stick to girl scouts Pogo! Leave those wild- woman alone!" Gene pulled two beers out of the ice and handed one to his blushing friend. Filling his plate with small sandwiches, Scott walked over to the big round patio table and joined his beautiful smiling wife. He winked at her as he put one of the sandwiches in his mouth. Susan watched him as he enjoyed his full plate.

"Gene, you won't be hungry for supper if you eat that pile

of sandwiches." She patted his knee and moved over closer to whisper "Or are you planning on skipping right to dessert again?" she teased.

"I could go for dessert first if you are my little cupcake!" he reached over and kissed her before diving into another small sandwich.

After everyone had eaten and the food cart and dishes had been carried back inside the ranch house, Gene looked around to make sure they were alone.

"Alright, has anyone seen or heard anything suspicious to report about on the staff? We need to start putting our heads together."

"We could have something. Speaking with both Vera and Maxine, we found each woman had things that stoked our interest." Jackie took a sip of her wine.

"Sounds promising. Let's start with Maxine Fletcher." Gene stood up to pull four more cold beers out and passed them to the men "Wine, ladies?"

"No more for me darling." Susan grew serious as she waited for her husband to refill her friend's glasses. "We believe, by what Maxine told us, that she was once a prostitute herself."

Michael got choked on his beer "Prostitute? Miss Maxine Fletcher, a prostitute? On which planet?"

"Mike, she really is a sad woman." Ali frowned at him as he was trying not to laugh along with James "Guys, this is not funny! Maxine said she was really pretty at one time and the top prostitute!"

"Pretty? How long ago, one hundred years?" James continued to laugh until he noticed the angry looks he was getting from each girl. "Look kids, serious, have you had a good look at that woman? She is…well…she's a dog!"

"James Tabor, That, is mean!" Susan stared over at her husband who sat smiling broadly at the tense situation between the girls and the guys. "Well, Gene Scott, are you going to say something 'cute' like, I wouldn't wear that face to a Halloween party?"

"Susan sweetheart" Gene reached out and caressed her cheek, as he laughed softly "I can see why Michael and James find her story hard to believe. She is not the most- friendly person I know. She is plain and homely looking, a little out of line for a hooker, don't you think?"

"Not if you were treated badly because you grew older." Susan's eyes softened "Maxine Fletcher has grown bitter from rejection and we think she might have been hooked on drugs."

"Drugs? Interesting!" Gene sat up "And what makes you think that?"

"It was what she said before she clammed up and left our room in such a hurry." Jackie finished her wine and set her glass down "She said she was hooked…and that is when she froze up, said she was bothering us with nonsense and left. I think there is more to Maxine's story but I don't think she will confide in us again."

"That's a start. What do you know about the cook, Vera Simon?" Gene lend back in his chair to wait their answer.

"She knew we were not Joe's girls." Ali propped up on her elbows "After asking her how she knew Joe's ladies, she said everyone in Greystone knew all the women working at Joe's Beauties. Vera casually stated the women did not stay in the big house all the time, but they went out shopping and dining like everyone else in town."

"Knowing Mrs. Simon had a lot of sons, Susan asked if any of them ever gave Joe any business." Jackie ran her fingers through her dark hair "In her jolly way, Vera said if they had they would never tell their mama, but they were all healthy men."

"I think Vera knows her sons do business with Joe's hookers." Susan reached for her husband's hand "She just doesn't want us to know what they do."

"What about Horus Hampton? Do you fellows have

105

anything on him?" Jackie waited for the four men to answer.

"He does a lot of ease dropping. That's way obvious." Michael stood up and stretched his arms, yawning "I think Hampton is just nosey."

"You do not know anything about Horus, do you?" Ali stood up, hands on her hips, looking at their blank faces "None of you! I guess it's up to us ladies to find something on dear Mr. Hampton."

"And just what are you planning to do, babe?" James put his arm lazily around Ali.

"Lover boy, I am not sure yet, but when the three of us put our heads together, we can do wonders!" Ali smiled with confidence.

"Like how you put your heads together and decided to surprise us as hookers?" Gene's eyebrow went up "And by three, means my Susan will be involved, so this little plan better be safe!"

"Scott, even though we would like nothing more than taking the credit for coming up with us becoming prostitutes, we really owe that brilliant ideal to our pimp, Phil." Jackie gave Gene a genial smile "You may thank him."

"Thank him?" Scott narrowed his eyes at Pogo who was forcing a shaky grin. Gene reached over and gently slapped his head "Real brilliant for a guy that likes girl scouts!" then Scott turned his attention on Susan and pulled her into his arms "Do not try anything stupid, young lady. The boys and I will handle the rough stuff, get it?"

"I'll be a smart girl. You can bet on that!" Susan smiled and looped her arms around his neck in a hug.

Chapter Eighteen

Reverend Gene Scott had gotten up early as usual and sat by the big window in his bedroom that looked out at the rose garden. In his lap lay his well-worn bible he had been reading since dawn. He closed the cherished old bible, whose pages were ragged from much reading, and gazed out at the rising sun.

"Lord, you have given us another beautiful sunrise. I wonder how many of your children will rise up early enough to enjoy it?" Gene ran his fingers through the curls that lay perfect on the back of his hair, "Lord, please get me through another day and guide my path. Help me control my temper when it comes to that rude mouth, Joe Stallington. Please be with my little babies while we are apart from them. I know their mama worries about them even though she acts brave." Gene closed his eyes prayerfully and took a deep breath. "And Father, please keep watch over Susan when I'm not able to. You know how much I love that girl. Amen.

Gene stood up and made his way out the door. The big house seemed quiet as he went down the stairs. He felt his stomach rumble.

"I hope that sweet, jolly, little chubby cook is up. I am starving!" he mumbled softly to himself as he walked up to the kitchen door and overheard Mrs. Simon speaking on the telephone. The preacher froze outside the door to listen, hoping his stomach would not growl and give him away.

"Joey, I tell you, Mr. Clint is who he says he is, a rich oil man who loves the ladies." She seemed to be listening to her caller when she laughed out "Oh yes, Joey! Mr. Clint has been wonderful to work for and he appreciates my good cooking! As I said, he loves the ladies and he really knows how to treat them, real special! He is a real gentlemen!" she listened briefly then continued warmly "Alright son, I will keep my eyes and ears opened, but I can testify honestly, Mr. Clint is the real deal." There was a brief pause while the other party talked "Alright Joey and tell your brothers to call their mama sometime. Goodbye son, I love you."

Gene walked through the kitchen door whistling as he winked at the surprised cook.

"Good morning Vera. Is this Joey, you have been talking to, your boyfriend or one of your sons?"

Vera took a relief breath as she broke into a toothy grin "Mr. Clint. You scared the begibbers out of me! How long have you been listening?"

"A-ha! So, it is your boyfriend, you, sly woman!" Gene pinched her chubby cheek "I guess that means I'm out of luck in hooking you!"

"Go on with you, Mr. Clint!" she giggled like a schoolgirl, blushing "Joey is not my boyfriend, he is my eldest son, always checking on his mother."

"Good boy!" Gene walked over to the coffee pot and poured himself a cup "You said you had seven sons. Do they all live in Greystone?" he took a sip of the steaming coffee and smiled "Great coffee! You know, if any of them are looking for work, I will be hiring soon."

"That is mighty kind of you, Mr. Clint, but all seven boys are employed here in Greystone. They are all doing fine." Vera pulled out a large iron frying pan and placed fresh sausage patties in it. After they begin to sizzle, she smiled up at the tall handsome preacher.

"My oldest son, Joey, has a thriving business in the heart of town, buying and selling to almost everyone living here. Two of my sons, Johnny and Tommy, work for him." Vera flipped the good smelling meat over in the pan "Billy is the next to the oldest and serves as the sheriff of Greystone with Jamie and Toby, who are his deputies." Lifting the brown sausage out, she immediately poured beaten eggs into the hot drippings and moved them around to scramble them. "Now my youngest son, Teddy, is a big lawyer in town and stays busy working for Joey and other wealthy citizens of Greystone."

"My gracious, Vera, no wonder you're so jolly. It appears all you son have done well." Gene took the filled plate of food and winked at the smiling cook "Vera, this looks wonderful! I say their loss is my gain though. Your sons have got great jobs but I got their great cook!"

Vera Simon chuckled loudly as he walked through the door to the breakfast room.

After eating his early breakfast alone, Gene walked quickly out to the big garage to get the Mercedes.

"Well Joe, or is it Joey?" he laughed to himself as he got behind the wheel and started the motor "I think the time has come for me to make a deal with that creep!" Gene drove the car away from the big ranch.

Susan walked quietly to the library to return the book she had borrowed the day before. Just as she was about to enter, she heard an unfamiliar voice talking to someone on the phone. The voice was low and seductive. Slowly, Susan peeked inside the door and could see the back of Maxine Fletcher. She stepped back from view, then paused to listen to the conversation between the homely looking housekeeper and obviously a man on the other end.

"Now sweetie, you know I am a really good judge of character, especially when it comes to men. I tell you, Mr. Walters is exactly who he claims to be, an extra wealthy oil man with a taste for women and drugs." She listened quietly to the caller "He is perfect, darling. The man is rich and thirsty for everything we have to offer. I say, when he comes calling, give him anything he wants."

As Susan lend in, hoping to hear Maxine speak the name of the person she was talking to, obviously in love with, when she felt the book she was holding suddenly slipping out of her hands. Susan closed her eyes, aggravated with her clumsy attempt to catch the falling book as it hit the floor with a thud. Making a face of self- defeat, she reached down and picked up the book and walked inside the library door.

Miss Fletcher waved for her to come in as she preceded in her conversation, only this time, she was speaking in her housekeeper's voice.

"Yes Mildred, I'm quite happy here. Mr. Walters is very well mannered and you might say, extremely friendly to the staff. Yes dear, I know he loves the women, but I do say, what red blooded man doesn't." she laughed "By what I can tell, I think the women enjoy Mr. Walters as much as he does them." Maxine Fletcher paused to listen to the other person "Yes, that's right! Have a good trip dear and we can talk when you get back. Tootle-loo." She smiled as she rung up the phone.

"That Mildred does like to chat. I try to call her between my cleaning jobs." The housekeeper picked up a feather duster and started dusting a row of leather books.

"So, this Mildred, is she some kin to you, Miss Fletcher? A sister maybe?" Susan pretended to scan the bookshelf.

"She is my dearest friend. We own a house together in town. A small flat on the west side." She gave Susan a small smile, then continued to watch her as she searched the long row of books. "This is the first time I am required to live in the employer's home. I usually work in the town of Greystone but return to the flat when I'm finished with my day's work."

"I am sure Lucky is glad to have your services, Miss Fletcher. It is a very large home for one woman to clean, but you do an excellent job." Susan pulled a book from the shelf "This one looks good and not too long to read." She smiled shyly at the busy maid "I hope I didn't disturb your phone call when I clumsily dropped my book as soon as I got down here. I really need my coffee to wake up and…I guess my mind was wondering."

"Disturb me? Heavens no, child." Maxine seemed to be relieved "It was time to get off that phone and go back to my work."

"Have a good day Maxine, and try not work too hard." Susan walked casually out of the library and to the stairs. She glanced back to be sure she wasn't being followed, then she turned and raced up the steps to Gene's room, just to find it empty. "Gene Scott, where are you?" she whispered as she walked over to the big window and looked across the courtyard to the double garage. She instantly noticed the big black Mercedes was missing. Susan frowned as she flopped down on the king size bed.

"Reverend Scott, I will just sit right here and wait for you mister!"

Chapter Nineteen

Gene Scott knocked on the red door and forced a big smile at Joe Stallington when he opened it, somewhat surprised to see the rich oil man waiting alone.

"My goodness Lucky, back so soon and might I add, so early?" the owner motioned him inside the quiet house. "Normally I would still be in bed at this hour, but I have a delivery coming this morning."

"I'm sorry to barge in at this hour Big Joe, but it seems my luck is not so lucky after all! I have a slight problem that you might help me with." The undercover preacher chuckled.

"Problems with that little cutie?" Joe slapped his back "I will be more than happy to make a swap for you."

"I just bet you would, old man." Gene pulled up a chair and sit down "So we are straight Joe, I do not have any plans of giving up my little young fox! The fact is, Roxanne has got a very bad sunburn from too much pool fun yesterday and she needs some time to heal."

"I get it!" Joe laughed out "She screams every time you touch her hot sexy body? How terrible for you, my dear friend."

"That is the reason for my visit this morning, buddy. I want to set up a date with one of your girls and if you have the stuff we talked about, work something out there too."

"You don't give up, do you friend?" Joe motioned for the maid to bring in the portable bar "If it's not too early in the morning, would you care to join me in a Bloody Mary?"

"Thank you for the offer Joe but I think I'll pass this time. I've got work waiting in the fields this morning." Gene Looked at the painting on the wall beside him, a naked woman stretched out on a red sofa, then smiled at the owner "That's some painting! What do you say Joe about my request, is it a deal?"

"I can tell you this much Lucky, I know the right girl for you among my beauties." Joe walked over to the painting and let his fingers dance over her breast "The girl I speak of has put in a request for you when you came back in."

"You don't say!" Scott gave the owner a broad smile "I didn't know I had a fan club!"

"She tried to talk you into taking her the first time you came in. You might recall running into the shapely blonde yesterday on our shopping street." His smile was conspiratorial "A real sexy dish, would you agree?"

"What red blooded man wouldn't, pal!" Scott's eyes twinkled with pretense "I remember her alright, only I didn't exactly run into her shapely body, she twisted her way right up to me. I recall she was showing off a lot of her talents."

Big Joe laughed as he lit a cigar and offered one to Gene. He took one of the expensive smokes and put it in his shirt pocket as the owner took a big drag before continuing.

"Her name is Candy and she is one of my best girls. Believe me Lucky, you will be very pleased with Candy."

"I do have a sweet tooth for candy!' Gene Scott winked and stood up "What about the stuff Joe, do I get it?"

"Let's see how things go with you and Candy, my friend. If Candy likes what she sees and approves your performance, then you're in Lucky." Joe stood up.

"Shit! Sounds like I just got lucky again. Who needs a four -leaf clover with my kind of luck!" Scott turned toward the door "Seven o'clock, tomorrow night?"

"That sounds terrific. Now if you rather come tonight instead, I'm sure I can arrange it, my friend." He patted Scott's muscular arm, feeling his obvious strength. "Making out tonight with that delicate baby doll could prove awkward. You don't want to hurt that hot chicks sunburn, do you Lucky?"

"I don't want to hurt her feelings either! She promised me a good night regardless of that damn burn!" Scott opened the door and stepped outside in the fresh morning air. Facing the street, he waved over his shoulder "See you and Candy at seven tomorrow night." Climbing behind the wheel of the Mercedes, Reverend Scott headed for the ranch.

Susan had pulled a chair up by the big master bedroom window to watch for her husband's return. She spotted the long black Mercedes coming through the massive iron gates. Jumping up, Susan raced out of the room and down the stairs. After looking around, she made her way quickly to the rose garden. As her husband walked across the courtyard, Susan gave him a low whistle and saw him stop and look around for the noise.

"Lucky, over here!" Susan motioned when he looked her way and harried over. Gene could read excitement on her beautiful face.

"What is it? You look like you just swallowed a canary!" his eyes caressed her shapely body as he pulled her inside a row of roses.

"Oh Gene, I thought I would jump out of my skin waiting for you! Have I got some great information on Maxine Fletcher!" Susan took a deep breath.

"Well, lets have it!" Gene patted her head as he admired how beautiful she had come with excitement "Then I will share some news of my own with you."

"Great!" she smiled, ringing her arms around his strong neck "I overheard Maxine talking on the phone in a very sexy voice to some man. She was telling him he could trust you, in so many words. 'Our' plain and proper Miss Fletcher, was calling this mysterious man, sweetie and darling. She was saying some really nice things about you until..." Susan bit her lip and made a face "until I accidentally dropped my book outside the library door."

Seeing the concern on Gene's handsome face, Susan quickly added "Do not worry, I covered my butt beautifully. Unfortunately, Maxine started speaking in the voice we all know and pretended to be speaking to someone named Mildred, whom she claims to own a small flat on the west side of town.

"Susan, are you absolutely sure she didn't suspect you in overhearing her real conversation with this mysterious man?" Scott looked worried.

"Like I told you, I covered my butt! I apologized to Maxine for dropping my book when I reached the library. After telling her I hadn't had my coffee yet and my mind was wondering. We had a friendly little chat and Maxine went back to dusting." Susan smiled, feeling proud of her discovery.

"Good girl!" Gene looked around to make sure they were still alone "Have you seen Horus anywhere this morning, sweetheart?"

Jackie and Ali had him go with them to the pool area, to get it ready for today." Susan laughed softly "I think poor old Horus don't realize he's being grilled."

"Let's hope not." Gene pulled her closer to him "I too heard a conversation this morning between Vera and her son Joey."

"Joey? Could that be Joe?" Susan's eyes grew wide.

"Smart girl!' Gene chuckled "Vera was telling 'Joey' all about me and I got a passing grade from mama."

"Did you get caught?" Susan patted his cheek "Or were you as smart as your brilliant wife?"

"Just as brilliant as my beautiful smart wife! I ask that chubby little cook if the Joey I heard her talking to was her boyfriend. I informed her I had heard her remark, I love you Joey!" Gene put his arm around her slender shoulder and pulled her even closer.

"Hey mister, where were you just now?" Susan pulled away and stared up at her husband. "You didn't even take Michael or James with you!"

"I did not need them tagging along with me. I went to Greystone to pay Joe a visit and make a date for tomorrow night." Gene laughed as he held down Susan's swinging arms.

"Gene Scott, I thought you were going to wait until you figured something out!" she whispered as she narrowed her eyes.

"I did wait and I have figured something out, my feisty little darling!" he whispered back "I will be taking Miss Candy to bed…" Gene grabbed her and held his hand over her mouth as she squirmed in his arms. "but…I will be making love to you!"

"Me?" Susan looked confused "I don't understand?" Susan placed her hands on her hips, still skeptical "Just how does this little plan of yours work?"

"Just stay quiet and listen to me." Gene put his hands firmly on her shoulders and looked deep into her blue eyes "First, I need you to pretend you have a very bad sunburn which you got at the pool yesterday. Anytime I touch you tonight, you act like you are in pain. A slight scream or two could help convince our audience."

"I can pretend I have a bad sunburn. That will be easy enough." Susan relaxed and gave him a weak smile "Go on."

"Tomorrow night, while Roxanne is tending to her sunburn, I go to Joes at seven o'clock and get to know Candy."

"Not too much I hope!" Susan stiffened back up at the thought of her husband being close to another woman "Do I know which one this 'Candy' is?"

Scott smiled in a teasing manner as he bent in to whisper "You did meet her on the street." Gene laughed as he grabbed her bawled up fist "Yep! She is the blonde you almost decked."

"Oh! That's just dandy! That blonde bitch making out with my husband!" Scott quickly placed his hand over her mouth.

"Calm down Susan and listen to me. After I take the flirty blonde upstairs, we will have a few drinks to get acquainted." Susan rolled her eyes in discuss and made a face at him. Reverend Scott laughed and continued "Then I will slip a little sedative in her drink and she will fall into a deep sleep."

"It's starting to sound better. Go on." Susan relaxed again "How do I fit into your little plan?"

"You and Pogo will be waiting outside in the back. If my calculations are correct, all the hooker's bedrooms are on the back of the house. I will open her window and light a cigarette. That will be your clue that it's safe to come up." Gene winked at her bright smile "Pogo will drive the truck so the ladder will fit. He will help you climb up and wait for you at the bottom to keep watch."

Gene took Susan's face into his hands and spoke tenderly "Sweetheart, this part is very important. All those bedrooms are bugged so Joe can hear everything that goes on between the client and the hooker.

"Why, that dirty old man!" Susan frowned.

"Susan, this man sells women like one might rent a car, he uses them for his own personal sex, so spying on them comes easy to the damn creep!" Gene looked around to make sure they were still alone. "Big Joe will be hearing everything we are saying and doing, Susan, so we must make him believe you are flirty Cathy."

"I get it." Susan smiled "I talk low and sexy, like miss blonde witch and we make wild sex! Old Joe Stallington will get over heated!"

Scott laughed out "Little darling, I know there is no cameras set up, so the creep will be listening extra close. He wants Miss Candy Apple to say I passed the test for drugs."

"Gene, if she is asleep through all this hot sex, how can she possibly pass you?" Susan face was plank.

"Look Susan, women like this believe what you tell them. They do not want you to think they can't remember because they got drunk. When she comes to, I just start bragging to her about our hot sex under the sheets and she will go around bragging to the other hookers what a great time we had!"

"It sounds like a good plan darling. Almost fun!" she

giggled "What happens if she wakes up while we are making love?"

"Easy! I plan to tie her up, blind fold her eyes, plug her ears, and gag her mouth shut!" Scott took his wife's hand "Then if she wakes up, she will think I'm a kinky bondage lover! Otherwise, I will be sitting in a chair, dressed, having a cigarette and brandy when she comes to. Just as long as my girl is on her way safely back to the ranch, I can wait and brag, then come home."

Susan hugged his waist "So you will fill Pogo in on all the details? Where are you getting the sleeping pills?"

"To answer both my girl's questions, I will get Pogo up to date and George Martin is supposed to have the pills already." Gene made a face "If that idiot does not start preaching to me about drinking with fallen women!"

"You can handle Reverend Martin, darling. In the meantime, I will go ask Vera if she has any remedies for sunburn." Susan laughed "Are we on or off for tonight, Lucky?"

"We are defiantly on, woman!" Gene patted her backside "I promise to be careful with your sunburn, but when I get into you, I might forget."

"I will try not to scream too loud, Lucky darling, you hot stud!" Susan waved over her shoulder as she walked stiffly away, pretending to have a bad sunburn.

Gene Scott chuckled as he watched the woman who had his heart, walk painfully away.

Chapter Twenty

"Martin, hand over the damn pills!" Scott whispered, hand outstretched "I do not have all night!"

"Seriously Scott, you might want to rethink this. A man of God going into a house of sin." Martin looked around to make sure no one was listening, "And to do business in that place! It just, well, it's just wrong!"

"Martin, you are about to get your stupid mouth mashed!' Gene Scott gritted his teeth in anger "That is why I am the one in charge here, Martin, instead of you! You think you can pray your way into making these stinking law breakers confess! This is the real world, Martin! To catch a jackass, you have to act like a damn jackass!" Scott stuck his head down in front of the shaken preacher "Now hand over those damn pills before I knock the shit out of you!"

"Alright Scott, O.K.! You do not have to get violent, for God sake!" he reached nervously inside his pants pocket and pulled out a small brown bottle "Let's just hope putting those drugs into alcohol does not kill that foul woman!"

Scott grabbed the pills and stuck them in his pocket. "Well, shit Martin, that's a chance I'll just have to take! Now I am going to have to rush through my shower to get back down here for the gathering time. Go ahead and serve the drinks but ask Vera to wait with the refreshments." Scott stormed out of the meeting and up to his room to change.

Susan checked her watch, then looked back up the stairs. Everyone else was enjoying their drinks when she finally saw her husband, standing at the top of the staircase. Suddenly her heart did a somersault as she watched her Reverend Scott make his way down toward her. Her eyes melted on his black silk shirt, opened halfway down, revealing his perfect manly chest. He wore matching black silk pants, which fit him perfectly.

Gene Scott's attention was on his beautiful wife, where she stood gazing up with her perfect luminous blue eyes. To add to her exquisite charm was the elegant, royal blue gown she was wearing. It made his heart beat fast in his broad chest just by taking her hand in his. The feeling they shared never lost its magic. Even though the other ladies sat admiring the handsome preacher, he had eyes only for the woman that held his heart.

"Roxanne, you look absolutely breath taking this evening. How is that sunburn?" Gene had noticed Vera and Maxine had come in to serve while he was still at the top of the stairs, so he had to stay in his roll as Lucky until he and Susan went up.

"Now don't you worry, Lucky; I do not think my sunburn will get in our way at all tonight." Susan took a sip of merlot, then touched his hand "Could I get Haywood to fix you a drink, handsome?"

Smiling down at her, Gene took her hand and walked over to the bar where the other preacher had regained his emotions after having a glass of wine before anyone came down.

"You may pour me a glass of the merlot, Haywood." Gene turned to the rest of their group and held up his glass "I would like to make a toast, to a very hot time tonight under the sheets!"

George Martin had just poured himself another glass and took a big sip just as Scott gave his toast. He got choked from the preacher's bold toast as Vera, unseen by everyone, winked at a smiling Maxine, who was trying hard not to laugh at the stiff butler. The other two couples clinked glasses with everyone as they shouted

"Here! Here!" Each knowing what lay ahead.

"Lucky, Vera has made some really groovy refreshments this evening. I will be happy to fix you a plate, if you like." Susan smiled over at the happy cook.

Gene bent down to whisper in Susan's ear "I am hungry, but not for food, my little chocolate drop!"

"Oh Gene, you remembered!" Susan whispered and took his strong hand "Our junk night on the ship!" their eyes locked briefly as they remembered back to happy memories. "But you might need to keep your energy up and I really know you are dying to dig in Vera's dream table!"

"Let's fill up the food tank then!" Gene pulled Susan over to the buffet table and loaded his plate. "We can join the others and you can help your big man eat this food!"

Gene and Susan walked over and joined their friends. Jackie couldn't take her eyes off the handsome preacher dressed like a model.

"My, my, Lucky! Don't you look dashing! Like a character out of a romance novel!" Jackie heard her boyfriend grunt. She reached over and patted his hand "You always look sexy, Dave darling."

"My slim Jim is always 'hot', but Tracy is right, there's something about you tonight that catches a girl's eye Lucky. Looking at you, stud, could make the female mind wonder into a what if…" Ali noticed James was frowning over at Scott. She smiled and took his hand "Relax Jimmy! You're the only man I need!"

Gene Scott was flushed with embarrassment as he cleared his throat "Alright ladies, I really appreciate all the flattery, but don't you think you're stretching things a bit far?" he took a big sip of wine after his last bite and turned to Susan, who was frowning over at her two friends.

"Foxy Roxie, are you ready for a little hanky-panky?"

Susan gave Jackie and Ali a faux smile and pushed her chair back and took Gene's hand.

"Hanky-panky sounds perfect, with you Lucky, you, sexy man! Any day!"

Gene laughed and stood up, looping his arm around Susan's shoulders. She yelled softly, then gazed up at him sheepishly "That…well, that hurt a little. Do you mind if we just hold hand going up the stairs?"

"I'm sorry sweetheart." Gene chuckled softly as he took her hand "I promise to be extra gentle tonight."

"Thanks Lucky. You are quite the gentleman." Susan winked at her husband as they made their way up the steps. She could feel the stares they were getting from the group below as she continued her act. "Watch that Lucky, that hurts! Oh! Not there!" Susan sighed as she spoke in a relieved tone "Oh yes, right there is wonderful!"

Scott mumbled loud, so everyone could hear him "But Roxie, that's your head for the love of oil! How in the shit can I make love to you if the only thing that isn't sunburn is your head?"

"Use your imagination!" Susan giggled to herself and ran into the big master bedroom.

Gene Scott quickly followed and shut the door behind him. "Use my imagination! Come here, you, little smart ass!" he picked her up in his strong arms and kissed her. They stood looking in each other's eyes, passion building as his lips found hers again in a fiery kiss. Still focusing on her awaiting lips, Gene undone her dress and slipped it over her long black hair.

As Susan watched him undress her, she continued her performance with a soft scream when he unsnapped her bra and threw it in the chair by the window. Smiling, Gene caressed her young firm breast.

"Nice scream, Mrs. Scott." He gently rubbed her nipples as she let out a soft sigh.

"Gene darling, take off your clothes, please."

He laughed mischievously as he slipped out of his silk shirt slowly, then laughed again when Susan pushed his hands away, and undid his zipper, as her eyes held his.

"Allow me, Reverend." Susan pushed his pants down to the floor, where he stepped out of them. "Now, take off those boxers, mister!"

"My pleasure, young lady!" Gene breathed heavily in her ear as he slid out of his underwear and toss them up in the air. Susan giggled at his clowning as they stretched out on the big bed.

Letting her hands glide slowly down his back and come to rest on his solid rear end, Susan could feel her man's growing need as he filled her with his complete manhood.

They lay wrapped in each other's arms until Susan whispered softly "I'd better round up my clothes and get back to my room."

"Damn!" Scott pulled her tighter in his embrace, not wanting her out of his sight. "I cannot wait until I get you home to our bed!"

"I know how you feel, darling. The sooner we can wrap up this mission, the faster we can get back to being Reverend and Mrs. Love Birds!"

Giving each other one more passionate kiss, Susan climbed out of the bed to get dressed. She blew Gene a kiss then walked out into the dimly lit hall.

Chapter Twenty-One

The next day seem to fly by making Susan nervous about the night's capper. She had excused herself earlier, telling everyone she was going up to her room to treat her sunburn with an ointment Vera had made for her. Susan had made it plain to the entire house, that she felt bad because Lucky had given her the night off and made plans to go find sex with another hooker until her sunburn got better. She insisted she did not want to be disturbed by anyone and closed herself behind her bedroom door.

Gene had told Susan earlier that it would look better if Michael and James stayed home with Jackie and Ali for apparent reasons. Neither one of their girls had a sunburn.

Susan checked her watch. It was time for her and Pogo to go. Checking her reflection in the mirror, she smiled at the simple tie around dress for easy removal. Susan knew going up the ladder might be a challenge with no underwear on, but she would not have time to undress, once with Gene.

Susan made it quickly from the house and down the dark driveway where Pogo was waiting beside the red pick-up truck. His eyes took in her skimpy outfit, clinging to her shapely body.

"Wow Susan, you are a knockout!" Pogo smiled shyly and opened the door for her. As he walked around to get in Susan thought

"Surely Pogo can't tell if I have no underwear on?"

"We got to get going, Susan. Scott left about thirty minutes ago." Susan smiled and nodded and Pogo speeded down the road to town. Reaching the big three- story mansion, Pogo drove quietly around to the north side, where dim lights glowed from each window above them. He stopped the truck on the grass and the only light they had was the moon shining through the big trees. Pogo got out and looked up at the lighted windows, trying to imagine all the action going on behind the closed curtains.

"We'll just stay here and wait for Scott to give us his signal. I will put the ladder up and help you get started. Then when you and Scott have …finished with…" Pogo blushed "Well, you know. I will help you back down to the ground and we will make a bee line out of here before we get caught."

Susan glanced over and saw him blushing. She stood on her tiptoes and kissed his cheek.

"I guess you feel left out, don't you?" she turned her attention back to the lit windows above them and swallowed back her nervous feeling. "There are so many windows to so many rooms up there! I just hope I go in the right one!"

Gene Scott sat in a large red plush chair as he looked around the empty sitting room. A set of double doors opened and Candy came waltzing in.

"I'm sorry it took me so long, you, sexy devil!" her slim fingers took the glass of brandy Scott held out for her as he began to put on his big performance. Starting at her head, Scott took in her well- developed figure, wearing an extremely tight black dress.

"I must say, you are very tempting, Candy. It was well worth the wait!" Gene faked a smile as his attention was drawn to her push-up bra effects. He chuckled as he thought, the slut is really trying to seduce me. "I must say, Candy, the girls are coming out to welcome me! They are promising me great times tonight!"

"You are a sexy devil, Lucky." She took a sip of her strong brandy and licked her red lips. "Hum, Joe has pulled the good stuff for us, handsome. I can see with our chemistry we are in for a 'hot' time tonight!" still in six-inch heel, the prostitute had to lift herself up to kiss him.

As Gene held up the full bottle of brandy to refill the

hooker's glass, he was glad his jealous little wife couldn't see what was going on inside this parlor.

"Can I freshen up your drink, doll?"

"You certainly may, handsome, but not down here. Let's move this party upstairs to my room, where the action is." Candy grabbed two clean glasses and made her way up the winding staircase, glancing behind her as she wiggled her way to the second floor. She stopped in front of a large white door trimmed in gold, opened it and smiled "Welcome to Candy's candy dish, sugar."

Her seductive flirting was making Gene feel queasy and uncomfortable as he watched her shut the door and lock it with a big gold key. She made her way to his side and ran her hand down his chest before laying the gold key in an empty dish on a dresser.

"We don't want anyone disturbing our fun tonight, Clint darling."

"No one except my wife." Gene was thinking. He forced a smile and chuckled "No, we would not want any company, you hot dish!" taking the glass from her hand, he set it down to refill. She draped her heavily perfumed arms around his strong neck and kissed him, then gazed up in his blue eyes.

"Would you like to undress me Lucky, or would you prefer I strip for you, slow and sexy?"

He smiled then walked over to fill their glasses with the strong brandy. As she made small talk, Gene slipped the sleeping pills into her full glass. He faced her, his eyes twinkling with mischief as he handed her the glass and held his up.

"Stripping sounds great beautiful, but first, you little fire engine, drink this down and I will do the same."

Holding the glass up to her red lips, she laughed "Why Lucky, are you trying to get me drunk? It would take more than this, darling. Hot Candy can hold her liqueur, sugar." To prove her point, the brazen hooker turned up her glass and drank down the contents. "Now take a seat Handsome and enjoy your drink as you watch a real woman perform."

Candy turned on some soft music as she began moving to the seductive sound. As she danced, the well -practiced - prostitute began removing her clothes. She was about to remove her underwear, when she sank, unconscious to the floor.

Gene Scott silently set down his glass, walked over to lift the unconscious woman up and lay her on her bed. He pulled the cloth from his coat pocket, along with the ear plugs, and tied her securely before stepping to the window and opened the curtain enough for Susan and Pogo to see him when he lit the cigarette. Then he continued his talking as if the hooker was still stripping for him.

"Damn Candy, you are one hot mama!" Gene pushed open the window and lit a cigarette, then continued with his wolf's remarks. "Get you sweet ass over here!"

Pogo looked up and smiled "Middle room, the biggest! Alright Susan, it's show time! You're on!" Helping her get started, Pogo watched her go quickly up the tall ladder in the dark and disappear through the open window with the aid of two strong hands.

"You sure are one sexy broad." Gene winked at his wife.

"I'm glad you like the merchandise, sugar!" Susan lowered her voice to sound more like Candy. And Scott tried hard not to laugh. Frowning, Susan hit his arm "Well, Lucky, what are you waiting for? Drop those pants! Little 'hot' Candy is waiting for some action!"

Gene turned and stared down at the sleeping woman, eyes covered, mouth gagged and tied securely. He felt anxious, as he moved his hands nervously behind him. Susan realized the situation made it hard for Gene to feel turned on, so she quickly untied her dress and let it fall.

"My, Mr. Walters, I don't believe I have ever seen a man so well endowed!" Susan's eyes were seductive when Gene turned quickly her way and noticed his beautiful, sexy wife standing naked in the soft moonlight. He could feel his pulse rise quickly as he yanked off his clothes and made his way over to her, pulling her into his strong arms. Susan reached down to collect her prize. "Lucky, you, Lucky man, stick that very long, very hard rod inside before I rape you!"

Gene Scott slung Susan to the floor and climbed on top of her. She let out a soft sound of pleasure when he filled her with his complete love. The passion was wild and demanding and with great emotion they both reached a fulfilling, fireworks!

"That was…" Susan took a deep breath "The hottest sex I have ever had!"

They lay, staring at one another, the sweat running between their hot bodies. Gene got up close to her ear and whispered

"Susan, shit, you really turned me on woman! I couldn't control myself! I love you!"

"I love you too, Gene." Susan whispered, still out of breath as he helped her up and with her dress. He looked around and found no underwear "You won't find any stud." She winked at him "Hookers don't have the time for such things."

He kissed her with passion and helped her out the window as he whispered to Pogo down below.

"Keep your eyes shut pal, my girl is coming down!" then he turned to his true love "I am sure we turned Joe on with that hot performance so he's probably looking for a free whore about now, unless Mrs. Stallington is available." Gene chuckled and helped Susan on the ladder "See you at the ranch, darling."

Scott sit sipping on brandy and smoking a cigarette when the drowsy hooker sat up rubbing her eyes.

"Well, sleeping beauty, you decided to awake after I wore your wicked sweet ass out!"

"Did we…did I…?" Candy looked down at her naked body, confused.

"And I must say Candy, you really gave me my money's worth!" Gene stood up and laid a hundred dollar-bill down on her chest. "A little something extra for all the 'action'! I look forward to the next time." Gene retrieved the key from the dish and walked to the door and unlocked it "You just lie there and rest, I can see my way out."

"Lucky, it was really wonderful, wasn't it?" she laughed and tried to smile normal "You are really hot yourself, stud!"

"I am glad you were pleased with my very long, very hard…" he winked "You, little she, devil."

"The bigger the better, Lucky!" she blew him a kiss, convinced they had indeed had hot sex "I still feel all 'hot' inside, real sexy sugar. If you like, we can go one more time, on the house!"

"I think you wore me out tonight! Sweet dreams, Candy." Gene opened the door and walked out. He did not feel at ease until he was outside, In the fresh air. He glanced up at her window "You, sinful little bitch!" he mumbled as he got into the Mercedes, his thoughts turning to Susan and the vision of her standing naked in the moonlight. His lips melted into a genuine smile.

"Damn Scott, my sexy little wife really got me horny tonight and fast!" he laughed to himself "What a woman!" Gene headed the car toward Susan.

Chapter Twenty-Two

Gene Scott got up early the next morning and woke James and Michael.

"Get a move on fellows, we have got a meeting in the west field!"

He walked out as the first rays of sun were coming over the horizon. Michael and James climbed lazily in the truck Scott had driven around to the side entrance. Yawning, still trying to wake up completely, James felt his stomach growl.

"No breakfast this morning, Scott? Who is so important we have to skip the most important meal of the day?"

"First, sleepy cat, we will have our breakfast when we get back." Gene turned the truck on a narrow dirt road "Second, we have a meeting with the Fed early, to keep it a secret. Third, we are about to wrap up this capper and the next time I go back to that whore house, I will be buying drugs, not a cheap woman!"

"So, last night went well?" Michael looked out the side view window to watch the dust flying up behind the red truck, then turned to see any sign of the Fed. "Did you and Susan have any trouble doing it? You know, in front of that bimbo?"

"Look Mike, even if we did or did not, do you think for one minute I would tell you?" Scott's eyebrow shot up.

"We heard it was very 'hot' sex, Scott!" James stared casually from the windshield "You became a wild animal!"

Gene Scott hit the steering wheel with discuss. "Damn! I know you did not hear this from Susan!" Gene gritted his teeth as he wondered what else his young friend saw when Susan went up and came down the ladder. "That damn Pogo!"

"Come now Scott, Pogo is an impressionable young man. Besides, he looks up to you. You are his role model." Michael fell back on the seat, relieved when the federal agents came into view "Fed ahead! Saved by the law!"

"Very funny, Mike!" Scott stopped the red truck and all three got out and walked up to the serious looking men lending against a long black car, unmarked. Gene's attention went to the one in the middle. "Oil strike! Fish in the pond!" Gene said firmly.

The man in the middle tipped his hat as he stuck a pipe in his mouth. "Drill oil! Bait the pole!" he smiled broadly "Reverend Gene Scott, I finally get to meet the dynamic tough get-the-job done Scott! I am honored, sir!"

"I seem to stay busy. I must be doing something right!" Gene stretched out his hand "Good to meet you. I think you can bring your men in pretty soon."

"We will put a bug on you and move in before things get out of hand." The agent motioned for a short bald man who had a small device in his hand. He placed it inside Scott's shirt to show him how it fit without being detected. "It is state of the art, Scott. There are no wires to show and it brings out every sound around you."

"It's too bad he wasn't wearing it last night!" James whispered over to his smiling friend and Gene Scott turned angrily to glare at him.

"My sources tell me you will have visitors this morning. The sheriff and his coons, not to mention his crooked lawyer brother." The agent patted Scott on the back "The name is Warren, Agent Tony Warren."

"It's good to finally meet you too, Warren." Scott smiled slyly "I think your man H.H. is keeping close tabs on my staff." He smiled broadly as Agent Warren shook his head.

"Nothing slides by you, does it Scott?" the agent pulled a paper from his pocket "Vera Simon has seven sons, all of which have this town in the palm of their hands. Over half the people living in Greystone are part of their scam. The rest of the good citizens are afraid to cause trouble, knowing several have dared to go against them and ended up missing. This is a mean bunch we are dealing with Scott, so I have called in more help!"

"Well Warren, I plan to go after Joe tomorrow night!" Gene Scott rubbed his empty stomach when it rumbled "I'm going in, with or without your men, so you better shake ass!" He walked over to the truck and opened the door, Warren right behind him.

"Scott, we need to wait for everyone to get here and in place!"

"Burnside waited for everyone. He waited for the union army to get there, to cross the Rappahannock River into Fredericksburg, to be in place before he took the town! Look what it got him, Mr. Warren!" Gene Scott climbed in behind the wheel "Just get your men here and in place! I want to wrap this damn case up and take my wife home!"

"Your wife?" Warren moved closer to the open door "I don't understand Scott. I thought your wife and family were in TarSa?"

"Looks like your plant is not as smart as we are, Warren." Gene cut on the ignition switch "Listen, I am a preacher! I would not ever take another woman to my bed! My wife is the only one I share my bed or my body with, got it!"

"But...what about last night, Scott? Are you telling me you were not making out hot and heavy last night in that whore's room?" Warren stormed out "I heard the whole damn thing for myself!"

"Shit! Double damn bugs, you and Joe!" Scott slammed his fist against the dash "Yes Warren. I was having hot and heavy sex in that sinner's bedroom! Some of the best sex I have ever had!" his eyes blazed "But damn it, it was not with that blonde bitch! I was hitting on my own wife, you eves-dropping bastard!"

"Now, now, Scott." Warren smiled, remembering getting turned on just by listening to the two lovers "We were listening for any talk about drugs from that Candy. I must admit, after listening to that 'hot' encounter between you and your sexy wife, we had to go inside and be customers at Joe's Beauties." Agent Warren winked at his smiling men "I'm glad it was a slow night! We each got a broad!"

"That's just 'great'!" Scott gritted his teeth "I am dealing with a bunch of sinners!"

"Shit, I'm sorry we missed it!" Michael slapped Scott's shoulder and received a growl from his big friend who started up the truck and threw the gear in first, then drove away, leaving the chuckling agents in a cloud of dust. Michael cleared his throat and looked at James nervously before speaking "Scott, say something."

"I cannot believe one beautiful act of love drove that many men to commit sin!" Gene's eyes blazed as he stared straight ahead. "A bunch of grown men getting turned on just from listening! Discussing! God, I hope Susan don't find out about our large audience!" he pulled the truck in the large garage.

"Maybe we will all feel better after we eat some breakfast and see our women." James climbed out and followed Scott to the front door. "By the way Scott, who is H.H.?"

Reverend Scott finally smiled as he slapped his thin friend's arm "Figure it out, brains." Then he got serious "Shit, I hope the little wife can't read my mind." Gene stopped and looked sternly at the fellows, who were trying not to laugh. "Don't either of you say anything about what you heard. Not to Jackie, not to Ali, and if you want to keep your teeth, 'never' to Susan! Is that clear?"

"Sure Scott, absolutely!" Michael smiled innocently "Our lips are sealed, right James?"

"I did not hear anything back there!" James tried to look serious and convincing "The secret is safe with me, Scott."

Susan and the girls were having breakfast when the men walked in and took off the western hats. The raven hair beauty smiled up at the man she loved.

"Good morning Lucky, you, handsome devil. Where did

you run off to so early this morning, and before having your breakfast?"

Gene noticed the cook listening carefully while she poured coffee for the three men.

"The boys and I were checking the north field for oil." Gene laughed as he picked up a crispy piece of bacon and took a big bite "Old Lucky can smell oil in the early morning light, especially when there is dew on the ground."

"Yeh, it's out there, just like Lucky said!" James filled his plate and flopped down next to Ali.

When Scott set his filled plate on the table and started eating, the round little cook walked back to the kitchen. Gene looked over at Susan and winked.

"Girls, how would you like to go horse- back riding this morning?"

"Horseback riding sounds wonderful!" Susan stood up and ran her hand playfully over her husband's curls "My sunburn is much better, but the pool is out. I do not want anything to keep me from you, Lucky."

James and Michael punched each other and laughed softly. It did not go unnoticed by Gene Scott. He frowned over at the two cut-ups as they continued to chuckle. He turned his attention to Susan and the other two girls who had stood up beside her.

"Go on up ladies and change into riding clothes, jeans or some comfortable pants." Gene watched the three women walked away, chatting about riding attire. His gaze fell on Michael and James as he slid his chair back. "Alright, you two funny guys, finish eating while you still have teeth!" Turning, Gene stormed out the room.

The girls made their way out of their room, laughing, until Jackie held out her arms for silence. Below them, standing in the far corner of the entrance hall stood Vera and Maxine, chatting like old friends. The three friends slipped slowly down the steps, hoping to hear some of their conversation. Just as they reached the landing, Ali sneezed loudly and startled the gossiping twosome. They quickly resumed their composure.

"My ladies, don't you look nice. Going somewhere?" Miss Fletcher ask politely.

"Mr. Walters has invited us to go horseback riding." Jackie put on a bright smile, despite feeling disappointed in getting caught. "It is such a lovely day. How can we refuse his kind offer?"

"Yes dear, Mr. Clint is a wonderful host. Now you three just run along and enjoy the ride." Mrs. Simon chuckled at the thought of herself trying to mount a horse. "that Mr. Clint sure is nice." The cook turned to face the housecleaner "As for you, Miss Fletcher, just stay out of my kitchen! I will clean it myself, plus the dining and breakfast rooms!

"You are on, Miss Simon! While you're at it, you are more than welcome to 'clean' your rooms on the third floor, that includes your bathroom as well!" Maxine Fletcher snapped back.

"That suits me just fine!" Vera put her hands on her robust hips "Just stay out of my way! You may eat my leftovers in the den, as well!"

"Gladly! The less I see of you, the better!" The maid forced a smile at the staring girls "I am truly sorry ladies, for having to witness our differences. Mrs. Simon and I cannot get along!"

"It's too bad you cannot be friends, seeing as to how you must work in the same house. You both do a wonderful job in your field, considering how large this house is." Susan gave a genial smile and waved over her head as she led her group to the door "We're off to the races! Come along girls, let's go round up those cowboys!"

The two spies watched the three beautiful girls walk away. Maxine took around Vera's large frame, smiling.

"Do you think those ladies heard us talking before that sneeze?"

"Those girls?" Vera Simon chuckled "They have one thing on their mind, my dear, satisfying those gentlemen. They do not wish to be swapped for another broad."

"Can you blame them?" Maxine put her arm around the cook's big shoulders "You are right, my friend. They could care less about our business. How about that cup of tea?" the two unlikely friends walked away chatting.

Chapter Twenty-Three

Gene watched as Susan, Jackie and Ali were making their way toward them, decked out in blue jeans and flannel t-shirts. His smiled showed his approval of their riding clothes.

"Ladies, what took you so long? I was beginning to think I had to send out the hunting hounds!"

"We got held up by a cozy conversation between two unlikely sources." Susan's voice was cheerful and bright.

"Let me guess," he whispered, "the cook and the housekeeper, right?"

"You are too smart for us Lucky." Jackie eyed Michael skeptically "Are you keeping some sort of secret from me, Handsome?"

"Who me?" Michael forced an innocent laugh as he stared at Scott "No beautiful, no secrets here. I'm just standing here minding my own business."

Martin walked inside from the front door and broke the tension by announcing "Mr. Walters, sir, there are four gentlemen outside who wish to see you."

"Oh shit! I forgot that sheriff was coming out." Gene motioned for the girls to go in the living room. "Wait in there, ladies. It shouldn't take long." Gene followed Martin out the front door, Michael and James close behind.

Four tough looking men watched the group come from the big house and walk their way. Their arms crossed, each man acted obnoxious in the way they lend against the police curser. The man in the middle straighten up as he tilted his big black cowboy hat.

"Mr. Walters?" Gene nodded and looked down at his badge. It was obvious to see he was the sheriff "I'm Billy Simon, the sheriff in these parts and we came out to welcome you to Greystone."

"That's mighty nice of you, neighbor!" Scott took his hand firmly and shook it "It's good to meet you, Bill." He looked over the rest of the unsmiling faces "Could these fine deputies be your brothers, Bill?"

"As a matter of fact, Mr. Walters, they are my brothers." The unfriendly sheriff forced a smile "The tall one to my left is big John. The short runt standing on my right is brother Toby. I wouldn't let his size fool you, Mr. Walters. I've seen him take down men your size if the law has been broken. We run a tight ship! No smart- ass thief can get away with a crime in our town! We can sniff out the troublemakers! Rest assured on that!"

"Then I best stay clean, right boys?" Scott chuckled, knowing he could take down all four brothers without getting one scratch. Scott turned his attention to the man in a dark suit "What is your job, undertaker?" he put on his mischievous smile as the straight face man reached inside his shirt for a business card and handed it to the handsome preacher standing several inches over him.

"I am Fred W. Simon, a very respectable lawyer in our town. I am with the law firm of Simon and Butler. If you ever need my services, feel free to call."

"I will keep that in mind, Fred, if I ever get into trouble with your tough brothers." Scott laughed loudly when the lawyer's face turned red "All of you are Vera Simon's sons, are you not?" Gene patted Fred Simon on the back as he continued "Your loss is my gain, fellows!"

"I beg your pardon?" the stiff lawyer reminded serious, triggering Scott to laugh even louder.

"Aren't lawyers supposed to unravel words? "You boys left your mother's nest so now I get her good home cooking. Your mama, her cooking…your loss! My cook, her great food, my gain!"

"Oh yes! Now I see what you meant." The lawyer speared on a faux smile "My mother is your cook!"

"Lighten up brother, Clint Walters appears to be a live wire." Bill Simon finally produced a genuine smile "Well Walters, we don't want to take up anymore of your time. I see by your horses waiting saddled and tied to your hitching post, you are getting ready to go for a ride."

"We thought we would take our guest out and show them some of my grounds." Gene Scott looked thoughtful toward the house "Please look in on your mother while you're here. I am sure she would love to see her boys."

"That's mighty kind, Mr. Walters. I'm sure we can take a few minutes to see her." Bill Simon tipped his hat "Have a good day."

"I plan on it." Gene motioned for Martin "Haywood, show these gentlemen to the kitchen and offer them something to drink. Tell Vera to take all the time she needs to visit with her sons." He waited until they were inside, then hurried to the living room to collect the girls. Silently, they followed the tall preacher out to where the horses waited.

Michael untied a white mare and led it to Jackie and held the reigns until she climbed into the seat. He looked at Susan and Ali "I know Jackie can ride a horse. What about you two girls?"

Ali walked over to one of the horses James was holding and climbed easily in the saddle "I've ridden ever since I was a kid. Jackie and I have been riding for years. It's been a while, but it's like riding a bike, you never forget."

Susan stared up nervously at the tall horse "Horses really look a lot bigger when you're standing right beside them!"

"Is this your first- time riding, sweetheart?" Gene put his hands on her tiny waist and lifted her up in the saddle. "Just keep your feet in the stirrups and move the reins like I show you. Try not to act afraid. The horse can sense fear and will try to dominate you instead of you being in charge of him." Gene climbed on the horse next to her and taught her how to move the reins, to turn left, right, to stop and start. "If you find

Prince trying to lower his head and eat a clump of grass, don't try to pull his head up using both reins, take one side of the rein and lift it up." Gene patted her leg "Ready? You can ride beside me, darling." He reached over and kissed her tenderly on the lips "You will be an old pro before you know it. I know how good my girl is at learning sports."

"Thanks teacher! I already feel like Annie Oakley!" Susan giggled nervously "As long as my hot sexy cowboy is riding the trail along next to me, with his big 'shot gun', count me in!"

Michael and James laughed, recalling the previous night's action between the two lovers. Gene shook his head with discuss as he bawled up his fist and gentle kicked his horse to start the ride.

The group of riders stopped under some shade trees and climbed down from their horses. Gene helped his wife down from her horse as she draped her arms lovingly around his strong neck.

"That is really fun when you get the hang of it. You are still a great teacher, Reverend Scott."

"I think so." He held her close as he kissed her tenderly.

"Let's watch that Scott!" James teased "We wouldn't want things getting out of hand!"

"Very funny, Tabor! Always the comedian!" Scott narrowed his eyes and motioned for everyone to sit down "Friends, this little cover-up is about to get wrapped up. It's obvious Vera Simon and Maxine Fletcher are spies. Can anyone shed light on Horus Hampton?"

"I don't think Horus is a spy." Susan looked around at the interested listeners "He is always listening to conversations, but not just on us. I have seen Mr. Hampton listening very carefully to Vera and Maxine. I have also taken note that Horus has nothing to do with them."

"Then what would be your guess, sweetheart?" Gene smiled, happy that his beautiful wife was getting so smart.

"Promise you won't laugh." Susan looked serious "I believe dear old Horus is working with us. An undercover F.B.I. agent."

Scott chuckled loudly and clapped his hands proudly. "Now, that's my smart girl! You are absolutely right!"

"Oh! H.H.! I get it now!" Michael looked up smiling, remembering Scott's comment to agent Warren "Your man, H.H. is keeping close tabs on the staff!"

"So that's what H.H. stood for." James slapped his friend's arm "I thought it stood for horny hooker."

"Look, you two, zip it up!" Scott made a fist and turned to the girls "We met the feds this morning before breakfast and they will be standing by to grab the crooked gang when I nail them." His serious gaze fell on the fellows observing him closely as he pulled out the listening device "The fed gave me this mic to wear so they can hear everything I am doing."

"And when he says everything, he means…'everything'!" James punched Michael's arm and Michael joined him in laughter.

"I hope you boys have a good dentist!" Gene Scott stared angrily "You are going to need him real soon!"

"Would someone tell me what the heck is going on between you three?" Jackie rose to her feet and took in the three men staring at each other. "There is something going on here, so out with it!"

"Jackie is right!" Ali joined her friend "James Tabor, spit it out before I send you to the dentist with a few missing teeth!"

"You might as well tell them Scott." Michael tried to keep a straight face "These girls want give up until you tell them."

"Tell us what, Gene Scott?" Susan jumped up and stood over her husband "Just what are you hiding from us?"

"Shit!" Scott slammed his fist against a nearby tree trunk and stood up over his beautiful wife "Susan, I did not want you to find out what happen. But these two morons just could not stop ribbing me!"

"Out with it, buster! Does it have anything to do with one of those men chasing whores?" Susan grew angry, thinking the worse "Tell me Reverend Scott, now!"

"Alright, I'd rather you hear it from me, Susan." Gene glanced over at Jackie and Ali "I swear, if either of you laugh, I'll strangle you!"

"Just spill it out, Scott." Jackie sat back down knowing she was about to hear some juicy secret from the handsome hunk.

"I cannot wait to hear now that you've got my curiosity up." Ali dropped down next to the beautiful brunette.

"Susan, when you came to Candy's room, you knew Joe Stallington had a bug in the room and could hear everything." Gene took her hand.

"Of course, I knew, you told me." Susan smiled "That's why we gave him such an outstanding performance."

Gene took a big breath and blew out "This is embarrassing to me sweetheart and I know it will you!"

"Go ahead, I'm waiting." She smiled and patted his strong hand "It can't be that bad."

"Well, maybe it can." He swallowed "Joe wasn't the only one listening to our performance darling, and I'm not referring to Pogo, who could hear everything we did as well!"

Jackie and Ali gave a soft chuckle and covered their mouth "Sorry Scott." They said in unison.

"Pogo…heard us? And someone else?" Susan felt flushed.

"As it turned out, the F.B.I. had an inside person place their bug in the prostitute's room. The entire department sent here were listening to everything we did and said. The head agent actually thought I was hitting on a hooker, until I informed him, not so nicely, I was making out with my wife!"

"Oh, good Lord! Gene! All those men could hear everything we said and the heated sounds we were making?" her eyes went big "Please don't tell me Pogo could see up my dress!"

"If he knows what's good for him, he had better have

closed those curious eyes!" Gene held her tightly.

"I could just crawl under a rock and stay there!" Susan's cheeks grew flushed.

"Got room under that rock for me, honey?" Gene tried to smile down at her.

"The best part is that those federal agents got so turned on by their hot love making, they stopped listening to go inside and buy some hookers!" James laughed, trying to picture the sex graved men crawling over each other, trying to get inside the whore house first. "Boy, I'm just sorry I missed all that excitement!

"Look stud, I don't think you need to listen to another hot couple in action to get turned on! You are already one hot lover!" Ali lend over to kiss James "Although, it would have proved fun to hear Scott getting it on!"

"We…had all that audience listening and they got turned on?" Susan looked into Gene's blue eyes "I knew it was really hot! I don't think I've ever seen you that excited!"

"Susan?" Gene blushed.

"Well, I say Susan, you go girl!" Jackie winked at her wide-eyed young friend.

"I did, twice!" Susan threw her hands over her blushing face "What am I saying? I know, the truth, but to blurt it out like that!"

"I'm sure it's just the shock of finding out you made that many grown men go crazy, Susan. "Jackie rubbed Michael's leg "Do you suppose our love making is spectacular enough to do that darling? Rats, and to think I missed that great performance!"

"How could it be any better than when we do it, sweetie?" Michael looked hurt.

"All I know is, Gene looked at me when I told him how well-endowed he was. He saw me standing there naked and dived on me like an animal in heat!" Susan laughed nervously at Gene's shocked expression "I knew I had to do something, darling. You were standing across the room, frozen, staring down at cheap Candy out cold. You couldn't get into the mood because of the situation or surroundings. I knew Joe would be wondering why things had grown silent, except for that sleazy music playing. I had to do something wild."

"And you did, my little Delilah!" Gene grabbed her and kissed her to stop her from further talking. "And not another word about our wild sex, young lady or I will share 'all' the hot details!" Gene chuckled when Susan lend against his broad chest and buried her face.

"I'm sorry, Samson, I couldn't control my loose tongue."

"Now, can we get back to the reason we rode out here?" Scott motioned for everyone to gather around as he sat on the ground, pulling his blushing wife down in his lap. "This is the plan: I go into Greystone tomorrow night to get a drug hit from big Joe himself. Michael and James, I want you to remain here at the ranch to protect our women, along with Pogo and Horus. I am pretty sure the four of you men can handle Vera and Maxine without Martin's help!" Gene chuckled and rubbed his hand gently over Susan's head. "You girls will be safe here and as soon as the fed round up this ring of law breakers, I will call in a couple of you boys to bring in those two women. Everyone got your orders?"

"Sounds like a good plan, Scott," Michael sat up, feeling anxious "but are you sure you don't want me or James to give you back up in case you run into some kind of trouble? They have seen us with you, man, and no one would get suspicious with one of your guys watching out for your safety."

"Thank you, Mike, but I've got this one!" Gene hugged Susan to reassure her look of concern "Don't you get all worried about me, little darling. You know your old man can get a job done."

"I know you can, Gene." She let her fingers glide along his handsome face "Promise me you will be extra careful! Just remember what you have waiting for you."

"That's what gets me through, Susan, knowing I will be coming home to your arms." Gene kissed her, pulled her up and led her to her horse.

Chapter Twenty-Four

Gene Scott stood staring out the window in his master bedroom, his thoughts deep in the task that lay ahead. If the owner of Joe's Beauties sold him the drugs tomorrow night, this mission would be completed and he could take Susan home to their family.

Susan walked quietly from the bathroom, wrapped only in a towel. She knew her husband was worried about the following night and could tell his mind was in deep thought. Her voice came soft and somewhat seductive.

"Reverend Scott, I really need your help tonight."

He turned to look at Susan, wearing only a towel and a coy smile. His lips broke into a genial smile as he went along with her game.

"Yes, young lady, do you need to confess something?"

"I'm afraid I do, reverend. I think I have been a sinful girl, sir. You see, I have been having sinful thoughts." She looked at him with so much innocents, Gene had a hard time controlling his laughter.

"Well my dear, I am a minister. Maybe I can help you. Just tell me what these thoughts are that have you so upset."

"In truth sir, you are the only one who can help me." Susan's eyes remind focused on Gene "I have been dreaming about you Reverend Scott. The two of us, alone on a deserted island, eating bananas and drinking spiked coconut milk as we make love all day long."

"I see why you think this is a sin, young lady." Gene made his way over to her and took her hands in his "You know I am a preacher, a man of God, not to mention, I am a happily married man."

"I know! I know!" Susan's eyes grew wide "But Reverend Scott, I need your body! I need to feel you hot with passion, pressed tightly against me!"

"Damn, you're good!" he swallowed as he straightened up "But my dear, I am a man of the cloth. I have made vows that must be kept."

"Alright reverend, you are right." She pulled the towel loose and it fell at her feet "I just want you to see what you gave up, Reverend Scott." Susan started to turned back toward the bathroom when Gene grabbed her back and pulled her into his arms.

"I just changed my mind, sweetheart!" Gene's lips melted over hers in a fiery kiss. Susan played with his wet curls as she whispered

"Take off those pants mister!"

Gene stepped back and ripped the shirt off over his head, then unzipped his pants and tossed them in a chair next to his big bed.

"I am waiting for the best part reverend. Do not keep me waiting!" Susan let her hand run playfully down his broad chest as Gene slung his boxers up in the air. He picked Susan up in his strong arms and tossed her on the bed. Rolling over next to her, Gene lifted her on top of him.

"Alright, you, sexy little siren, let that dream come true. Have your way with me!"

"Shit Gene, you're turning me on now!" with all the passion built up between the two love birds, bananas or spiked coconut milk could never compete with their incredible connection.

"Damn, life with you just gets better and better, Susan." Gene pulled her tight into his arms "stay with me tonight, darling. I think those two busy-bodies have stopped watching us."

"No arguments here Gene darling." Susan smiled sleepily and curled up in his arms. "Hopefully after tomorrow night, we can go home to our bed and our babies."

"That is what I'm praying for." Gene lifted her face and kissed her tenderly, then reached over to switch off the bedside lamp. "Sleep tight, beautiful."

The evening came quickly the next day as Gene gave out last minute instructions to James and Michael.

"Alright fellows, keep a close watch on our girls. This thing is about to get wrapped up and we do not need a monkey wrench thrown in to clog up my job!"

"No sweat, Scott." Michael whispered "We are going to set up the card table and ask the girls if they are up for a challenge against me, James, and Pogo. They are all very competitive about winning and showing us men up."

"Fine! Anything to keep Susan occupied." Gene looked up the staircase to see Susan leading the way down. "I would not want her deciding to help me at the last minute, understand? Whatever it takes, keep her here!"

"We dig it, man!" James smiled with complete confidence "We will keep Susan so busy, she won't even remember you're gone."

"Good luck with that, pal!" Scott smiled down at Susan's sad face when she stepped up in front of him. He spoke out, in case someone was ease-dropping. "Roxie, you are looking extra lovely tonight."

"Always for you, Lucky." Pulling his head down, she whispered "Are you going to town now, Gene?"

"Yes sweetheart, but I will make the deal fast, then the fed can come in and take over." Gene squeezed her hand gently "Do not try to follow me, Susan. You have a bad habit of doing just that and I don't want you near that place. Give me your word, darling."

"Oh, alright, I promise I won't follow you." Susan looked hurt and helpless "Couldn't you at least take Michael or James with you?

"Now Susan, it is all set." Gene bent down and kissed her "I need the guys to stay here and make sure my girl keeps her promise."

"Gene Scott!" she spoke softly as a frown came to her face. "I said I promised! It will not be easy but I will keep my word and stay right here, worrying!"

"Susan" Gene gently took her face in his strong grip "I am a big man. I can take care of myself, little darling. There is nothing for you to worry about. Just trust your old man."

"I do trust my man! It's the other jerks I don't trust!" Susan ran her fingers through the curls across the back of his head "Just hurry back! I will be waiting for you in your bed!"

Gene Scott smiled broadly, kissed her with passion and walked out the door humming their song, 'Chances Are'."

Michael checked his watch and noticed Scott had left for Greystone almost thirty minutes before. It had been long enough to reach town and the whore house. His blue eyes fell on Susan, who sat staring at her cards. Michael laid down his hand of cards and stretched his arms.

"How about taking a break from the game and fix some snacks and beer."

"That sounds perfect, Mike." Jackie laid her cards down as she looked around the table "Don't anyone touch my cards! I finally got a winning hand."

Everyone had turned their cards upside down and stood up when they noticed Susan still sitting, staring at her cards, lost in deep thought. Ali gently touched her shoulder to get her attention.

"Susan, we are off to raid Vera's kitchen! Come on honey and join us."

"If you don't mind, guys, I think I will go find a good book in the library to get lost in." Susan stood up, giving a coy smile "It might help stop me from wondering what is happening at Joe's."

"Alright Susan, we can understand your mind is not on your card game. Forgive me for peeking dear, but I did notice you were holding a straight set just now, the Ace of Spades!"

Michael winked at her blushing cheeks "Can you read in here if we keep our voices down?"

"If it's alright with you, I will take it up to Lucky's room and read it." She smiled as she picked up her unopened bottle of water "I told him I would wait for him there."

"Whatever makes you happy, you cool hot mama, but remember, do not go outside this house." James winked at Susan.

"James is right, pretty girl, we all need to stay in the house tonight." Mike always the gentleman, pulled the chair out for Jackie when she returned from the kitchen with a tray filled with snacks. Ali was close behind her carrying a six pack of cold beer for the gang.

Jackie sat down and patted Michael's knee as she smiled up at Susan "Susan, if you need us sweetie, just give us a shout."

"Thanks, you guys are the best!" Susan made her way to the big library to search for the perfect book to take her mind off her husband.

Switching on a lamp, she started scanning the full shelf in front of her. She pulled out a romance novel titled: Moon light Over a Peaceful Sea. Susan smiled as she remembered back to when Gene had almost kissed her in the moonlight on the ocean liner going to Africa.

"This book looks good and it may give me some pointers in making love." She spoke softly. In a dream like state, Susan turned to leave when she bumped into the dreary housekeeper.

"Maxine, you startled me! Slipping up behind me like that!"

"I am truly sorry, Miss Roxanne." Maxine Fletcher shut the library door and locked it with Susan unaware of her turning the key behind her back. "I saw you come in here and I need someone to talk to. I could never turn to Mrs. Simon and you always seen to care about people. I feel that I can trust you, my dear."

"You can trust me, Maxine. I really, truly care about others. I once had a minister friend who helped me to care for other's needs. What is it you wish to talk about?" Susan laid her book down and took the woman's cold hand.

"It's Joe, Miss Roxanne. He…he and I used to be…lovers." Maxine dropped her eyes as they appeared to fill with tears "It may be hard for you to believe dear, but I was his mistress for many years. I was young, sexy, beautiful and exciting. Then I got older and Joe started eyeing younger women, who surrounded him." The sad housekeeper cried "Miss Roxanne, I think Joe wants and desires you!"

"Me?" Susan's mouth flew open "Well, he can't have me! I belong to G…Lucky! Lucky and I are…well, Lucky does not want to give me up!" Susan put her hands on her hips in defiance "Who the hell does this 'Joe' think he is anyway? Running around on his wife! Breaking your heart and now has the nerve to think he can just have me!"

"Miss Roxanne" Maxine Fletcher's eyes grew dark and angry as she took a tight hold on Susan's arm "My Joe can have any woman he wants and he has his mind set on you!"

Before Susan could say another word, a hand holding a smelly wet rag covered her nose. Susan fault wildly with her assailant until she blacked out and her knees buckled under her. Tom Simon easily picked her up and carried her to the open doors leading outside the library.

"Coming Maxine! Your job is finished here!" the cold steel eyes fell down on Susan's limp body as he stepped out into the darkness, followed by Maxine Fletcher.

Chapter Twenty-Five

Gene Scott stood beside his car and took a deep breath then spoke calmly.

"Alright Warren, you had better have you men waiting because all hell is going to break loose."

Tony Warren frowned over at his second in command.

"What the hell is that Scott up to!" the agent stared at the speaker, hoping for more of an explanation on the preacher's intentions. He could only here the footsteps of the tall strong minister as he approached the big house of prostitution. "Just pay attention and get ready to move in!"

Scott knocked on the red door and slapped his big western hat against his leg. A thin butler opened the over- size door, smiling.

"Mr. Walters, do come in. Mr. Stallington is expecting you and is waiting in the den."

"Hopefully not the lion's den." Gene laughed with confidence.

"Not quite the lion's den, sir." The butler chuckled "It is Big Joe's dealing room, the place where he makes deals with men, such as yourself."

"A room set aside just for making deals?" Gene's eyes tinkled as he followed the thin butler down a dimly lit hallway to a red room. The walls, furniture, and drapes, were all red. Big Joe sat smiling in a red chair. "Shit! Joe, this room could be hell!"

"It proves to be for some clients, Lucky, if we don't see eye to eye." The robust owner's manner grew dark as he observed the big man's cool demeanor. "If you fail to pass our screening test, you could end up...let me just say, no one crosses Joe and lives to tell about it."

"You don't hold nothing back, huh Joe! Do I assume you

are talking about murder?" Gene gave him a faux smile as he took the cigar offered and looked around the red round room. "I certainly hope I passed that test, my friend. I wouldn't wish to spend my eternity living in a room like this!"

Joe Stallington broke into a cheerful chuckle as he stood up and slapped Scott's broad shoulders.

"Lucky! Lucky, you are a breath of fresh air! Most clients turn white when I tell them that in such a menacing way. Care for a drink, my friend?"

"That all depends, Joe, does it have poison in it?" Scott chuckled "I still don't know if I passed that test."

"Congratulations! You passed with flying colors!" Joe picked up a glass of expensive brandy and handed it to Scott. Picking up his glass, he held it up "A toast, my friend. Your performance was outstanding! You have the highest marks of any client in the history of our operations!"

"High marks, that's a relief!" Gene raised his eyebrows playfully "If you don't mind my asking, just how was I tested, Joe?"

"First, there's my dear mother, bless her heart, she adores you. I think it will be hard to convince her to leave your employment, so you can hire a real cook."

"Vera? Vera is your mother? Damn!" Scott pretended to be surprised by this revelation "Look Joe, maybe your mother could stay right where she is if she's happy there. Your mama really knows how to cook."

"Yes, she does, Lucky. She is the very best cook around. When mother is not spying for me. She acts as head cook here in the big house." Joe poured himself another glass of brandy and held up the bottle, offering Scott a refill. He waved it away, smiling. "No more? Afraid the law will stop you for drinking, pal? Not in my town, Lucky! I own most of this town and that includes the law enforcement. My friends get a free pass!" he lifted the bottle back up, smiling.

"That is very tempting, my friend, but I think I'll save my

brain for some of those good drugs when I get back home." Gene winked "Getting back to Vera, I can't get over that innocent sweet woman being a spy!" Gene shook his head in disbelief "So Joe, who is the second person to test this big guy?"

"Sweet, sexy, Candy! She gives you the highest grade." Joe took a big sip of the strong drink "I think I'm a little jealous of you, Lucky. My Candy tells me you are second best to me, but I believe the beautiful blonde is lying to keep me happy."

"She is a hot number." Scott stared at the big owner "Tell me Joe, are there any other spies you are going to take from my employment?"

"Perhaps one more, but for now, I know you came to purchase some drugs for your personal recreation." Joe set down his glass and rang a bell and instantly the thin butler appeared "Phillip, go get that package I prepared earlier for Mr. Walters." They both watch the butler walked away then Joe motioned to a soft red chair across from his.

"Please take a seat, Lucky, and I will explain how this deal will work. I will ship out to your ranch a case of the best drugs money can buy. Then each month, I will send another. I sent Phillip to get you a small amount to take with you today. It's a free sample of all the great drugs that will be in your supply each month." Retrieving a bill from his red jacket, he handed it to the preacher. "Does this price agree with you, Lucky?"

"It is very reasonable, Joe, if the drugs are as good as you say." Scott stood up and placed the bill in his shirt then extended his hand out to shake the pimp's hand. "Well, if that's all, I'll grab those drugs and shove off."

"Hold on Lucky, there is one more little matter we need to discuss." Joe looked at the adjoining room "Maxie, my dear, will you please come in and say hello to your previous boss."

Maxine Fletcher walked through the double doors, her long black dress cut low in the front, revealing her pushed up breast. White pearls surrounded her silken neck. The once drab slick bun a top the maid's head, was now swept up high and her make-up made her look some- what younger, even attractive.

"Mr. Clint" came her low sexy voice "I hope you will forgive me for spying on you, darling." Maxine ran her fingers through Scott's hair. "It really became a pleasure watching you with those whores. You really are a lady's man, handsome." She smiled, revealing white teeth against her very red lipstick. "If I wasn't so crazy over my Joe, I would snatch you for myself."

"Maxine, you are quite the actress! You are really very lovely when you're not dress like a depressed housemaid." Scott turned toward the red door "This has certainly been a day of surprises Joe, but if I can please have the drugs, I really need to get going."

"There is one more thing, Lucky. It's about Roxanne." Joe put his arm around his paramour.

"What about Roxanne?" Scott's voice grew loud.

"I know you have a thing for this little lady, Lucky but…" Joe smiled "so do I."

"That's just too damn bad! You can just forget it!" Reverend Scott's eyes shot fire "You cannot have her, Stallington, she is mine, damn it!"

"Now, now, Mr. Walters, this is my business and I can do as I please! I own these girls!" the robust man sneered.

"You OWN THEM?" Scott shouted "You treat them like slaves, you bastard! They are not a herd of cattle you can brand!"

"Oh Lord! Scott is getting angry! He is going to blow everything!" Warren's partner was sweating as he listened to the heated argument going on inside the mansion.

"Just cool it, Smith!" Warren hit the table with his fist "Scott, damn it, you have got this far, don't screw it up now!"

"Who the hell is this Roxanne anyway? Why does this hooker mean so much to Scott?" Smith looked up, eyes flaring with suspense.

"Scott is a preacher and these heathen jackasses are about to get the best of the good reverend." Warren patted his partner's back "Scott is tough, he will make it! By God, he better!" the federal agent pulled his chair up closer to the speaker and glanced over at Smith "By the way, that Roxanne girl, I think she is Scott's wife."

Inside, the argument continued as Big Joe stormed out "The girls get paid good money Walters! And by God, that is my business and I suggest you stay out of it! No hot shot rich man is going to tell me what I can or cannot do with my girls!"

"Don't you dare use God's name, you devil! Cheating on your wife with this…" Gene smiled mockingly over at Maxine Fletcher "this harlot!"

"Damn you Walters, Roxanne is mine! I will give you two…no three of my girls in her place!" his cold eyes stared wildly into Scott's.

"Like hell you will! I would not trade her for every damn whore you have Stallington, or is it Simon?" Scott's jaw jerked nervously "Now give me those damn drugs and get the hell out of my way!"

"Look Walters, it's too late, except it! She is mine!" he smiled slyly.

"Roxanne doesn't even belong to you Simon! She works for Pretzel or have you forgotten that!" Gene's eyes burned down on him.

"I will give Phil an offer he can't refuse." The arrogant man snapped his fingers and two strong men stepped through a hidden door behind Gene and grabbed his arms. "Now, my brothers will hold you until we settle this conversation!"

"I can guarantee you, Simon, Pretzel will never sale Roxanne to you, you creep!" Gene Scott felt the two guards dig their fingers into his arm. He looked down at their grip and faked at smile for each thug.

"Then he will be persuaded to sale her." Simon laughed sarcastically "And if he refuses, he will be eliminated, then I will own all three girls!"

"You are one filthy bastard, Simon!" Scott's attention was drawn to the double doors as Maxine pulled Susan into the room. Gene's heart sank when he saw his wife standing there in a see-through white dress wearing nothing under it. He could tell by her swaying and closed eyes, she had been drugged. It was at that moment Gene Scott's blood began to boil.

"You, sorry excuse of a human being! What the hell have you done to my woman?"

"There you go again Walters! Your woman?" Joe Simon's voice dripped venom.

"SHE IS MY WOMAN, DAMN IT!" Scott yelled.

Susan opened her eyes when she heard Gene's voice ring out. The room was spinning around her as she tried to focus on her see through dress. In a haze, Susan looked at Maxine, who resembled someone familiar, then she looked up at Joe, whose smile gave her the creeps.

"Where, where am I?" Susan finally looked around the round red room. Her body started to shake uncontrollably "Oh shit! Am I in hell?"

Gene Scott closed his eyes, his heart aching as he could feel his wife's fear. He turned his attention on the man's face he wanted to smash his fist through.

"Simon, you bastard! Don't you dare touch her!"

"What may I ask, can you do about it, Walters?" he had placed his misguided confidence in his brother's ability to hold the strong man in place. "The girl is mine, Walters! You might as well face the facts!" His lustful eyes fell on Susan as he pulled her in his arms "My little young Roxanne, all mine!"

"Take your disgusting hands off me right now!" Susan

struggled to get free from Joe's strong grip. "You are not my man, you pig!" she turned her head and saw Gene. She pulled her hand free and pointed "There, there he is! He is my man!"

Joe Simon yanked her around to face him "Not any more beautiful! You are Joe's girl."

"No! Gene, help me!" Susan jerked to free herself.

"Take your hands off her now before I kill you!" Gene yelled as his right elbow jabbed into Tom Simon's side and knocked him across the room. With his right hand free, the angry preacher grabbed brother Bob up by the throat and slammed him down hard on the floor. Hitting his head on a coffee table, Bob Simon blacked out cold.

Tom Simon, feeling dazed, struggled to stand up as Joe yelled out for help.

"Get him Tom! Teach him he's not as Lucky as he thinks, hot shot oil man!"

Gene turned to face the bodyguard, a sure smile creped upon the preacher's face and he motioned for him to come to him.

"Come on, little brother, show this big man what you've got!" when Simon charged him, Scott was waiting with his fist and sent the big brut back against the wall, this time knocking him completely out.

"Alright Simon, you are next! You, lousy bastard!" Taking three giant steps, Scott reached Simon, picked him up and threw him over the red sofa, and waited for a loud thud on the other side as the heavy pimp hit the hard, wooden floor.

Susan ran into Gene's strong arms. As he held her tightly, he called out to Simon.

"That will teach you to touch my wife, you bound for hell bag of rotten garbage!"

"Your wife?" Maxine Fletcher let out a scream as she ran behind the sofa and stared down at her lover "Joe, what can I do?"

"Call Billy now, and tell him to get his ass here fast with

the entire sheriff department!" Joe stood up and pulled a gun from his jacket. "Stay still Walters, or whoever the hell you are, or I will shoot your wife!"

"Look, you chicken-shit coward, why don't you fight me like a man!" Gene pushed Susan behind his tall frame "It's me you want, jackass! If you're so damn tough, come get me!"

"Gene darling, please don't get shot by that jerk!" Susan cried and laid her head on his broad back. Gene started laughing.

"My little woman is right, Simon! You are a jerk, a big fat, sinning, jerk!" Gene looked over at a wide- eyed Maxine Fletcher "And you, what kind of woman are you anyway? You are this married creep's mistress and yet you watch the fat bastard mess with pretty young women! You even help the rotten soul by getting him the young girl! Damn, you're just plain stupid or you don't give a shit!"

"I…I…Mr. Clint?" she mumbled.

"Scott! The name is Scott, you bitch!" he yelled, then turned his attention back on Joe Simon "Well, Chicken shit, come on, I'm waiting! Come near me with that damn gun and I will wrap it around your sorry head!"

Unaware of what had taken place, the thin butler came in behind Gene. He handed him the bundle of drugs and jumped, startled when his boss yelled out.

"Phillip! You idiot! Get those drugs back and get the hell out of here!"

The butler looked over and saw his boss holding his small revolver pointed toward the rich man.

"What…what should I do with them, sir?"

"Hide them, you fool!" Simon waved him toward Gene "Get them and go!"

The butler stretched out his trembling hand to retrieve the bundle from Gene's tight fist. Gene Scott smiled down at the nervous little man.

"Phillip, if you want to keep your teeth and the use of your damn arms, I suggest you turn back around and get the shit out of here!" Gene gently slapped his red cheeks "Be smart pal and do as I say."

The butler turned pale and took off running as Scott chuckled and held up the bag filled with the evidence he needed to bust this case.

"I've got everything I came for Joe!" Scott spoke loudly, knowing the fed were listening "I think your little game is over!"

"Well Scott, if it's over for me, then I am taking you with me, you stinking spy!" Joe Simon aimed the gun and caulk the trigger "See you in hell Scott!"

Susan screamed!

Chapter Twenty-Six

"No! No! Somebody, help!" Susan screamed out of desperation and before Joe Simon could pull the trigger to kill the brave preacher, Michael jumped him from behind and wrestled the fat pimp to the floor. Michael easily twisted the deadly weapon out of Joe Simon's hand.

Scared for her life and getting caught, Maxine Fletcher started to escape through the double doors but was soon stopped by James Tabor.

"My, my, Maxine, it's true what they say, a little paint can brighten up any old barn."

"Take your hands off me, you, skinny bean-pole!" Maxine stared up angrily at her outspoken assailant.

Gene walked over to the unhappy hooker, Susan lovingly wrapped in his arms.

"My dear Maxine, it's such a pity you got so fixed up just to go to prison and wear drab clothes again."

The federal agents opened the main door to the red room revealing all the hookers and staff in the big hall being handcuffed and read their rights. Warren made his way over to Scott as Smith handcuffed a frowning Joe Simon. The chief agent smiled up at the tall handsome preacher.

"Reverend Scott, you really did it! You cracked this case wide open."

"Reverend?" Joe's eyes grew wide "What the hell kind of preacher are you?"

"The best kind, you jerk!" Susan walked up to him, still in Gene's strong arms and stared at the defeated man "Gene gives the best sermons for holding an audience, he is the best missionary on the earth, and the church is lucky to have him because Reverend Scott gets the job done! Wouldn't you agree, Mr. Warren?"

"You said it Mrs. Scott, the very best at what he does. He can keep us on edge with his tactics, but in the end, Scott gets his man!" Warren chuckled.

"Thank you, Mr. Warren for seeing Gene's brilliance!" Susan stepped closer to the prostitute-drug salesman and placed her hands on her hips "And for your information Joe Simon, Gene is the best daddy in the world to our twins! Last, but defiantly not the least, Gene Scott is the best lover any wife would ever want!"

Gene stood back, arms folded in front of him, smiling from ear to ear as he listened to Susan throwing out compliments pertaining to him. He picked her up and kissed her.

"That's my girl!" Gene finally noticed all the men standing around, looking at Susan, wearing the see-through dress, her beautiful knock-out figure showing plainly underneath. His attention fell on Susan, who was looking up into his eyes, smiling. "Susan, sweetheart, maybe we had better find your clothes."

The group of men laughed when Susan quickly looked down at the revealing dress she wore. She jumped out of his arms and got behind his tall frame to hide herself. Gene Scott's eyes blazed on the gawking men as they tried to look round his big frame.

"If you fellows want to keep your staring eyes and your smiling teeth…" Gene faked a laugh "I suggest you get your ass out of this room, now!"

They quickly responded by leaving the room, knowing the strong preacher meant business after discovering the two beefy bodyguards belonging to Simon, unconscious. Tony Warren laughed as he started to trail behind his men.

"Warren?" Gene called out and the federal agent turned around, keeping his eyes on Scott's face instead of his wife's shapely body. Scott chuckled as he threw him the bundle of drugs "There's your evidence Warren! Now you have proof!"

The agent laughed as he threw the bag up and caught it

proudly, then walked away. Gene turned and looked down at a weeping Maxine Fletcher, hands secured behind her back. She looked up at Gene when she heard him say her name.

"Yes, Mr. Clint…I mean, Mr. Scott?"

"Just tell me where you put my wife's clothes, Maxine and I promise to behave like a gentleman." Gene took her shoulder and squeezed it "I'm waiting!"

"Her clothes are just inside those double doors." Her eyes grew dark "Just ask bean pole here!" Giving James an angry look she continued "I am sure he saw them when he crept up behind me!"

James had remained behind to hold Maxine, but he had immediately closed his eyes when Scott stormed out for the fed to leave or they would end up toothless and blind. To avoid feeling his big friend's wrath, he knew to restrain himself from staring at Susan in her revealing dress. Slowly, James pointed to the room behind him.

"Scott, you will find Susan's clothes hanging across a sofa."

Gene patted James' back as he smiled down at his eyes shut tight. He grabbed his wife's hand and took her inside a room that resembled a parlor with a floor length mirror in one corner. After closing the door behind them, Gene pulled Susan into his arms and smothered her with kisses. Smiling, her arms circled around his neck tightly.

"Oh Gene, my heart is still pounding! I was so afraid that devil was going to kill you!" the reality of what could have happened swept over her and she broke into tears "He…he almost pulled the trigger! If Michael hadn't stopped him…"

"Susan, my darling Susan! Relax, it's over, the bad people are going to prison!" he squeezed his arms around her and looked deep into her blue, wet eyes. "God, I love you, Susan! Today, tomorrow, and always!" his fingers ran over her perfect full lips.

"Lift up your arms, beautiful, let's get this dress off my

girl.!" As he pulled it over her head, his full attention fell on her naked body. Dropping the skimpy white dress to the floor, Gene pulled her up close to him. Closing his eyes, feeling the pleasure of having her against him, he smiled "We had better get you dressed before I lose control in here." Suddenly Gene realized he was still wearing the mic.

"Oh shit!" he reached inside his shirt and switched off the little red button "We certainly don't want to get those agents all hot again with no prostitutes available."

Susan laughed as she pulled her sweater over her head. Bending over, she scooped up the white dress and held it up toward her husband.

"Should I keep this hot little dress, darling?" she smiled into his blue eyes "Will it turn you on?"

"I don't need that dress to get turned on by you, little darling." Gene retrieved the dress and tossed it back on the floor. With a twinkle in his blue eyes, he pulled her in his arms "Besides, you wouldn't be in it long enough to need it!" the loving couple laughed and walked hand-in-hand toward the red door.

Chapter Twenty-Seven

Gene and Susan walked out of Joe's beauties for the last time. The scene that greeted them on the street was six white prison vans, loading passengers. The Scotts smiled at each other, then heard the familiar voice of the federal agent. Tony Warren gave Scott a thumb's up. Taking Susan's hand, Gene walked out to the agent.

"Warren, it looks like you've arrested over half the town!"

"Thanks to you, Scott!" Tony Warren motioned for one of his men to take over as he pulled the preacher to one side "That butler, Phillip, spilled the beans on everyone connected to the crime, for a lighter sentence." The agent chuckled "His only request was, to be protected from you, Scott."

"Smart guy." Gene saw Vera Simon waiting outside one of the vans loading women. The once jolly cook now held her head down, looking sad. Feeling an ache of sadness himself, Gene squeezed Susan's hand and walked over next to his former cook. Gene lifted her face gently and in a soft voice said "Vera."

Vera looked up in his sincere face, tears racing down her chubby cheeks.

"Oh, Mr. Clint…Reverend Scott, I truly am sorry. A preacher? I knew you had a kind heart. You are so different from all the other clients."

"My dear lady, what happen? Where did it all go wrong for you? I feel your love and devotion, your friendly, sweet manner." Gene took both her hands in his.

"I guess I got swept up into the business, Reverend Scott. It all started with my husband, Joseph senior, when he won the big house in a card game. My oldest boy, Joe junior, talked his daddy into selling drugs and prostitutes, when junior married the town hooker." Vera hung her head in shame "My Joe

165

molded each of our sons into what they became, but Joseph respected me enough to keep me out of the business. After his death, Joey decided I needed to move into the big house to be his personal cook. It wasn't long Joey had me spying on clients to find out if they were spies or undercover fed. Those suspected of being spies, simply disappeared." The sad woman wiped her eyes "I simply blocked out what my sons where doing with these people. I knew they were doing bad things, but…Reverend Scott, they are my sons, my little boys, and…I…love them."

"Vera, Sweet woman, a mother's love runs deep for her children." Gene wrapped his strong arms around his former cook in a hug. "I am sure if you pray for forgiveness, you find happiness and peace in your heart."

"As a young girl, I grew up in a Christian church, Reverend Scott. I do believe in our Lord's forgiveness." Vera's smile was warm as she reflected on her life "I guess I've just been loss."

"Vera, I will speak to the authorities on your behalf, to get you a lighter sentence." Gene took hold of her trembling shoulders and gave her a reassuring smile "I will also inform them about your good cooking and placing you in the kitchen while you're behind bars. At least you will be doing what you love and my guess is, you will be the head cook within a week. Trust me, I know a good cook when I enjoy their food."

Vera finally laughed and straightened up her short heavy frame. "Reverend Scott, I feel so much better!" she reached over and smiled at Susan who had been observing the caring gentleness of her husband. "And you, his little wife all this time." Vera felt the tight grip from the police offer who had walked up to load her in the van.

"I'm sorry lady, but it's time for you to get in and take a seat."

"Don't you be worrying, Vera, God will always be with you!" Gene hugged her one last time then gently kissed her cheek as he looked down at the young officer. "Take good care of this lady."

"Yes sir." Gently taking her hand, the policeman helped her up the steps then turned around to see another officer bringing a long line of women, their make-up smeared from crying. The unhappy blonde stopped in front of Gene and Susan.

"Lucky? Or is it, Scott? We…we never had sex, did we?"

"No madam, I never touched you!" Gene took Susan's hand when he noticed her staring at the hooker.

"Then, if it wasn't me Joe heard you making out with hot and heavy, who was it?" Candy narrowed her eyes at Susan, who stood smiling. "It was you! Roxanne!"

"Susan, her name is Susan Scott! You are correct, I made love to my wife!" Scott looked at the hopeless girl, knowing she and the other prostitutes would be serving many years in prison. "Candy, maybe you and your friends could use this time to turn your life around and start over. Repent of this sin filled life and change."

Candy stood tall as she brushed her hair back and laughed in the minister's face.

"Save your preaching, Scott! I will do my time in this rotten prison and then I will find another Joe to work for!" her eyes shot frost at Susan "As for you kid, you don't have what it takes to be a prostitute!" she laughed and climbed on the van before Susan could respond. Squirming, Susan tried to free herself from Gene's strong grip.

"Gene, turn me loose! Let me get on that van and straighten that bitch out!"

"Susan, sweetheart, let her go!" Gene spoke loudly "She is right! You are far too good of a woman to be a hooker!" he pulled her into his arms "On the other hand, you are one hell of an actress, my sexy little siren!"

Susan smiled up at her husband and relaxed as she watched some of Vera's sons being led up to a van behind Gene.

"Oh darling, look who is coming our way in handcuffs. It's your welcoming committee!" Gene turned around to see Sheriff Bill Simon, trailed by the lawyer, and two deputies. All four- brother's attention were trained on Gene Scott."

"Well, look here, it appears it's my time to welcome you fellows on a free ride to prison!" Gene Scott broke into a big smile "Don't you love it when the law wins!"

"Scott!" the crooked sheriff dripped with hate for the preacher who had stopped their operation. "We have been in business for as long as I can remember and we have always weeded out spies and done away with the stitch!" Bill Simon squinted his eyes and laughed mockingly "Then the great Gene Scott came waltzing into Greystone and tore apart our family business."

"Speaking about your business, looks like you boys were caught with your pants down!" Gene chuckled at his own remark "With all your prostitutes running around, it must have been hard to keep them up! Where you're going, you want be pushing women around anymore or taking advantage of innocent towns people."

"If I ever get out, Scott, I will hunt you down and kill you, you bastard!" Joe Simon walked up, escorted by two heavily armed police officers.

"You boys are a disgrace to your dear mother! Vera deserves a lot better!" Never taking his eyes off the leader of the organization, Gene spoke to the officers standing around "Take these heathen sinners out of my sight!"

As Joe Simon was stepping up on the van, he turned around for one last look at Susan.

"So, you were the hot little number in Candy's room, making out with this over- heated husband of yours." He smiled, lust in his eyes "Now I really want you in my bed, you little hottie!"

Gene jerked him up by his collar "Listen, you foul mouth shitass, if you don't shut up and get inside that damn van, I will kill you here and now, and rid the world of You!"

"You heard him threaten me! Arrest him!" Joe Simon shouted.

Tony Warren had been taking in the conversation and walked up between the two angry men. He jerked the prisoner out of Scott's grip and shoved the instigator up on the van.

"Look Simon, take a seat and keep your big trap shut or I will let Scott kill you here and now! Think of all the money we can save the taxpayers not having to keep your sorry ass up for the rest of your stinking life!"

Susan giggled and hugged her husband, who was smiling from ear to ear.

"I am glad we did not miss any of this, sweetheart." She pulled his head down and kissed him "Thank you for taking up for me again, darling. The nerve of that jerk!"

"No one will ever say anything bad about you, Susan, and get by with it, not on my watch!" Gene took her hand and headed for the Mercedes. Hearing a familiar voice call him, he turned around to find Horus Hampton's outstretched hand.

"Reverend Scott, you finally cracked this case! Now I can go back home!"

"Horus, you brought in Vera, I assume." Gene shook the undercover fed's hand.

"I did, but my job was quite easy compared to yours." Horus looked toward the women's van pulling away. "I almost felt sorry for poor Vera Simon."

"Vera will be find. She is one tough little lady." Scott patted the frail man's shoulders "Good luck and enjoy your family, Horus."

"Thank you, Reverend Scott, Mrs. Scott. Have a safe trip home." Horus Hampton picked up his old worn brown suitcase and headed for the bus station.

Gene whistled for Michael and James, who stood watching the row of vans pull away.

"Come on fellows, we are going back to the ranch and grab

some supper! I am starving!" Gene helped Susan inside the car as the two friends walked up "Soon as we eat, we can all pack our things and head for home tomorrow morning."

"That's hip with me, man, we will follow you." James winked at Susan and walked lazily to the red Lincoln town car. Gene frowned back at his flirting and drove the Mercedes quickly out of town.

Chapter Twenty-Eight

When the group of four walked into the ranch house, Ali and Jackie were making their way from the kitchen, laughing. They stopped when they noticed Michael and James had returned, along with Gene and Susan, all safe and in one piece. Jackie let out a long sigh as she grabbed Michael by his arm.

"I didn't know what was happening when Michael and James tore out of here and sped off toward Greystone!"

"That's something I would like to know myself, fellows." Gene gave the two friends a questioning look "How did you know I was in trouble and needed assistance?"

"After playing cards for thirty minutes, I noticed Susan did not have her mind on the game, so I suggested a short break." Mike ran his fingers through his thick dark locks "Susan ask to go to the library to get a book and wait for you in the master bedroom."

"After we had played a few more rounds, Mike ask me to go upstairs and check on Susan. I found your bedroom empty, so I ran down to the library thinking she had decided to stay in there and read. The door was shut, so I tried the doorknob and found it locked!" Jackie grew breathless "I pounded on the door, calling her name, but I couldn't get any response. So, I ran and got Mike!"

"James and I ran to the library and kicked the door open! The library was empty! Susan was missing and her un-opened bottle of water was lying on the floor!" Michael looked over at Susan, who had been listening, her eyes wide as she remembered what had happened. "The room smelled like either and the outside door was standing open."

"Do you remember what happened, darling?" Gene put his arm around Susan's trembling shoulders.

"I remember I was in the library and I had found a good

171

book to read until you came home." Susan reached up and traced her husband's lips with her soft finger "I was worried about your safety, darling, and I couldn't get you off my mind."

Gene pulled his wife in his embrace, gave her a loving hug and smiled deep into her blue serious eyes.

"Who showed up in the library Susan, Maxine?"

"Yes, it was Maxine Fletcher, with some story about needing someone to talk to. I realize now she was setting a trap for me, pretending to be hurt by her ex-lover, Joe. Then she said Joe wanted me, Roxanne! I said a few true remarks about her 'wonderful', lousy Joe, and the 'dear' lady became hostile and angry at me. That's when some strong ox grabbed me from behind and smothered my nose and mouth with an either soaked rag. I put up a good fight until the either got the best of me and knocked me out cold!" Susan looked up at Gene "The next thing I knew, I was swaying back and forth in a red room, wearing a revealing white dress!"

Pulling her tightly into his strong arms, Gene turned to Michael.

"Then what happen after you found Susan missing?"

"Then we went to find H.H. and told him everything we knew and we needed him to round up Vera and Maxine, thinking she was still here in the house, and bring them downtown." Mike recalled the urgent feeling to work quickly. Gene and Susan's life could be in danger.

"It was a tense feeling when we found Vera in the kitchen, but Miss Fletcher was obviously gone!" James' heart pounded, just remembering the nerve-racking moments before he and Mike dashed from the big house "That poor woman, Vera, burst into tears while repeating, 'O Lord, they took her! Why Joey, why? Mr. Clint really likes that little girl!"

"Without saying another word, I grabbed James by the arm and we drove to the whore house as quickly as we could!" Michael continued the story "We slipped un-noticed through

172

the back door and heard all the commotion, ran in to find Joe aiming that gun right at your chest!"

"Scott! Good Lord! You could have been killed!" Ali's eyes were wide in disbelief.

"Mike, what did you do? What on earth happen?" Jackie squeezed his hand nervously.

"I grabbed the gun and wrestled that shit-head to the floor!" Michael looked over at his hippy friend and laughed "My buddy grabbed the very tempting Miss Fletcher!"

"Miss Fletcher? Tempting?" Ali turned her lover around to face her "Spit it out!"

"Relax Ali, Mike is pulling James' leg." Scott grabbed his empty stomach when it growled "Our dull housemaid turned out to be a flashy hooker! Susan was right, she still is Joe's stupid mistress! The clueless woman didn't even seem to mind if good old Joe slept with the younger hookers." Gene look down at Susan, glad to have her safe in his arms "The creep even had plans to take my girl for his own private pleasures!"

"Just like that, take Susan? Why, that sorry devil!" Ali patted Susan's hand.

"I am sure Scott did not just hand her over to the overly heated rat fink!" Jackie frowned, picturing the heavy man with the red face.

"Gene was wonderful!" Susan smiled up admiringly into his handsome face "My Gene told that worthless piece of trash, in more than a few words, he would never have his woman!"

"Mike, would you stand up for me like that?" Jackie looped her arms around his neck.

"Let's just say, no man better never, think about stealing you from me, baby!" Michael bent over and kissed her as Scott shook his head and headed for the kitchen.

"Look fellows, I'm starving! Let's round up some food! Let's hope Vera left some leftovers in the refrigerator."

Pogo came from the kitchen, shaking his head. He was

wearing a bright red apron wrapped around his waist.

"Scott, you had me scared out of my mind, man! You could have been shot by that over-heated man! My life would have never been the same if you had got blasted away! Shit!"

"Pogo, pal, give it a rest and stop worrying. You know it's over because I'm standing here in one piece. But if I don't get something pretty soon to eat, I might drop dead from hunger!" Gene smiled down at the red apron, adorned with a big white daisy. "If you are wearing Vera's apron, buddy, I take it you have made supper?"

"Not just any supper, Scott!" Pogo grinned proudly "This is a big night! You, along with your fine group, have busted the prostitute-drug ring! Since this will be our last night here, before flying back home, I thought we should take advantage of this free food."

"That's a great ideal, Pogo! What's for supper?" Gene walked over to the wine cooler and pulled out a large bottle of champagne, then popped the cork. "Jackie, you and Ali grabbed eight glasses, we need to make a toast!"

"Champagne sounds wonderful, Scott! Pogo has made his famous baked spaghetti and it looks and smells terrific!" Jackie and Ali set eight champagne glasses down in front of the handsome preacher and watched as he poured. "Martin, Ali, and I made a beautiful salad and we set this romantic table, complete with candles."

As Michael and James lit the candles, they gave each other knowing looks of what lie ahead.

"Alright Pogo, get George in here! We are going to make a toast!" when the happy group were in front of Scott, he held up his glass "A toast, to the best group of actors I've had the opportunity to work with in my short career as a missionary-detective! To a job well done!"

The glasses clinked around the candle lit table and the happy group sampled the bubbly. After giving a short blessing, they dived into the delicious meal. After enjoying two helpings, Gene sat back and stretched his long arms.

"Pogo, pal, you just keep getting better with this cooking!' he stood up and started stacking plates "Alright gang, let's get this mess cleaned up and start packing!"

"Start packing? Tonight?" Michael stood up and pushed his chair under the table "After a romantic meal like that? You have got to be kidding?"

"Kidding? Me kidding?" Scott reached for an empty tray and started stacking the plates on it "No Mike! When I say start packing, I mean just that! Start packing! We are leaving for home first thing in the morning, bright and early!"

James took Ali's hand and walked toward the door "Scott, baby, you can pack tonight, that's hip! I, for one, will get up a little earlier to pack in the morning, man! I am taking my chick upstairs to hit the sheets, daddy-o!"

George Martin blushed and rushed off to the kitchen with the empty baking dish. Jackie laughed as she watched the preacher disappear behind the door, then she smiled over at Gene Scott.

"Look Scott, the four of us will get up at sunrise and pack our things. We know the drill! Up early, packed, ready to go, eat and run!" she gracefully took Michael's arm "These lovers are going up now to make hot wonderful sex! Happy cleaning up!"

Gene watched the two couples walk up the steps all hugged up, then he rolled his eyes in discuss.

"That leaves the four of us to clean up this mess before we pack for home."

"No, you don't Scott! You and Susan had a busy and trying afternoon." Pogo pushed his big friend toward the staircase. "You two love birds fly on up to your nest and if Susan were mine, I would wait and pack in the morning too."

"Thanks for doing the dishes buddy. Be sure Martin helps you. He has had it easy around here." Gene took his young wife's hand "And unlike the rest of these sex starved kids,

Susan and I have responsibilities waiting for us at home! It's pack, to bed, up and at 'em, bright and early!"

"Whatever you say Scott!" Pogo watched as they climbed the steps. Pogo smiled when he noticed the minister's eyes fall on Susan's rear end. He mumbled to himself as he turned toward the kitchen "Sure Scott, like you are just going to pack and go to sleep! Ha!" Pogo made his way into the dining room and retrieved the tray Scott had stacked up, then glanced back and whispered

Everyone has a woman, except George Martin and I'm not sure he even notices women." Pogo's eyes lit up with a bright ideal "When I get back to TarSa, I am getting me a woman! I will call sexy Gloria Ann Weber and have her under my arm before I tell Scott!" Laughing at the ideal, he headed toward the kitchen, calling out "George, get out here and get the rest of these dirty glasses and silver wear! I'm washing, so grab a dish towel!" he past the red- faced preacher with his armload.

When the Scott's walked inside the master bedroom, Gene walked over to a closet and pulled out his suitcase. He called over his shoulder as he opened the one piece of luggage.

"Susan, you can go to your room and pack your things." Gene looked over and winked "Then you can come back and sleep with me."

"Sure thing, darling." Susan watched as her husband pulled his clothes off hangers and began folding them. She smiled to herself "Gene, do you mind if I take a short shower first, sweetheart? I can still feel those Simon brother's hands all over my body and Joe's terrible cigar smoke in my hair."

Gene stopped to look over at his beautiful wife, waiting for his reply.

"Sounds like a good ideal honey. It might make you sleep better. Enjoy a good clean shower!"

"Thank you, darling." Susan pulled off her clothes and threw them on his dirty clothes pile. She noticed she had her husband's full attention as he watched her.

"Just leave your clothes there with mine when you're finished, honey." Gene swallowed "I'll have room in my laundry bag."

"You are so sweet." Susan turned and made it a point to walk slowly to the bathroom, smiling to herself and thinking "Pack your bags, Gene Scott? At least you can see what you're not getting tonight!" she stepped under the warm water.

Gene stood staring at the bathroom door. He could feel his growing erection in his pants.

"Damn! That little Delilah!" He yanked off his clothes and threw them on top of his wife's clothes. He slipped into the bathroom and up behind Susan. Smiling, he grabbed her around her tiny waist.

"Shit! Gene Scott!" she yelled softly "You scared me!"

He laughed mischievously and whispered in her ear "I thought I could wash your back or something."

"Something?" she laughed and handed him her soapy washcloth "You may scrub my back, Reverend Scott!"

"My pleasure, Mrs. Scott!" he rubbed the soap over her smooth back and threw down the rag. His strong hand ran up and down her back until they slid around to the front, where he grabbed her breast. "I think I will wash these beauties too."

"It does feel like you are…doing a good job, mister." Susan breathed heavily when she felt him press his body next to hers. She could feel his excitement when she turned to face him, soaping up her fingers and moving them all over his tan body. Gene pulled her into his arms and started kissing her with fiery passion. His breath grew heavy as he whispered close to her ear.

"My love, my Susan, today, tomorrow, and always, I will give myself only to you, darling!" reaching around her, Gene cut off the shower and swept her up in his arms then carried her to the bed.

Susan smiled down at their dripping bodies as she ran her

fingers through his wet curls.

"Gene, my darling, we are not on our honeymoon here. We do not know who will come in and clean the room after us."

"Susan?" Gene continued to kiss her with passion "I don't really give a shit who cleans up after us! I need you, now!"

"Then take me Reverend Scott!" she kissed his neck "Fill me up with your love, darling, now!"

He laid her down and moved down over her. Gene was so aroused he could not control his body and when Susan pressed up against him, they both let out a soft sigh of pleasure.

Gene Scott lay, holding Susan close, not wanting to let her go, but knowing they must get their rest and be up early to travel home. He brushed the hair gently from her eyes as he kissed her nose.

"We could change these sheets and no one would know two fish made love in this bed."

"Great ideal, handsome!" Susan laughed and slid out, pulling Gene up with her "I did not wish to sleep on wet sheets anyway."

Laughing, Gene and Susan took off the wet sheets and replaced them for a restful night. Susan reached for her robe.

"So, it's pack now, Scott? Then up, eat and head out!"

Gene grabbed her and pulled the robe off, smiling."

"Get your butt in this bed, young lady!" Scott climbed in beside her and switched off the lamp "New plans! Sleep, get up early, pack, eat, and then we can roll those wheels!"

Chapter Twenty-Nine

The Scott team drove away from the Lucky C Ranch for the last time and decided to leave through the town instead of taking the long road out. Greystone's streets were line on both sides with the happy citizens. They all began cheering and clapping as the two cars drove slowly passed them. Pogo watched from the back window of the Mercedes like an excited child.

"I feel like we are in a parade, grand marshals or someone important!"

"Look at the smiling crowd! I guess they finally feel free!" Susan returned their waves and smiles.

"It feels pretty good to see all our hard work has paid off." Scott noticed an elderly man waving him down as he walked out to greet him. He pulled the car over to the curb and put down the window "Looks like the entire town as come out to see us off, brother."

"Reverend Scott, there are not enough words to express our gratitude to you and your fine group for everything you have done to clean up our old town." Tears came to the old mans tired eyes "The people of Greystone have selected me to offer you our thanks and give you this gift."

Gene took the brown envelope offered him and opened it slowly. Inside he was surprised to find, a cashier's check for $500,000. The humble preacher glanced up in his rear- view mirror at the car Michael was driving, then he glanced back at Pogo and looked at Susan, who were both still caught up in the excitement. Susan looked down at the large amount written on the check, then back up into her husband's smiling face. Gene winked at her, then turned and handed the gift back to the old gentleman, who stared down at the brown envelope containing the big sum.

"What is your name?" Gene reached out and touched the frail hand.

"Floyd Austin. I was the mayor of our small town until Joe Simon appointed one of his crooked friends." With trembling hands, Mayor Austin tried to hand the check back to Scott. "Please reverend, take the money. The citizens of Greystone got it together as a thank you for saving our town and giving it back to us. I wished it could more."

"It is more than generous, Floyd, but the way I see it, the best way to save all these fine folks is to restore that old run-down church at the edge of town and open back its doors again for worship and praise! All of you should be thanking God for His saving grace. Our group is just His instruments. God is our conductor, He leads, we follow!" Gene Scott climbed out of the car, knowing the crowd had grown silent and had heard his words, so, he continued.

"Listen friends, please take this money, each of you gave out of love, and rebuild God's house! In return, God will rebuild your faith! Worship and sing His praises! Each and every one of you must pray! Pray for guidance and always include giving thanks for everything God has done for you. His heart will be full of joy, that His lost children have returned and you will have his grace and perfect blessings of peace and love!"

Gene bent down and look in the car at Susan. He smiled broadly when he read the total love she was feeling, as tears laced her beautiful luminous blue eyes. Scott stood back up to face the mayor of Greystone.

"I will speak to my bishop when I return home, Floyd. The Methodist church will send a building team here to help you rebuild Shady Grove Methodist Church. If I recall, that was the name on the weathered beaten old sign tangling between two worn post, covered by an overgrowth of vines."

"Reverend Scott, when our church is finished and the doors are open once again, can we count of you to return to our small town and bless us with your presents for the first service?" Floyd Austin held on to hope "I know the town's citizens would be honored to hear you preach on that first Sunday."

"It would be my pleasure to come back and help you fine people celebrate your first Sunday of worship at Shady Grove. The church will be sending your new minister as well to join me, along with their family. I'm sure you will give them a warm welcome." Gene shook his hand and waved at the adoring crowd "May God bless each and every one of you!"

Climbing back inside the Mercedes, Gene drove away from the town of Greystone, followed by the red Lincoln Towncar.

Michael and James said their goodbyes after stepping off the plane at the TarSa Airport, as they waited for their luggage to come around.

"I hope we can have another adventure soon, Scott! Things are a little slow and quiet around here." Michael shuffled his and Jackie's luggage as he watched his girlfriend walk toward the gate, talking to Ali and Susan, her small overnight suitcase in her free hand.

"Just give us a shout Scott, if you need our services man!" James looked down at Ali's heavy suitcase "Shit, women! It's a good thing I'm stronger than I appear."

"Just remember James, those women of ours depend on us to be real gentlemen. You fellows try to be good and act like true gentlemen." Gene chuckled "At least, be careful You don't want to get on the wrong side of either of those three! I'm not always around to help get you out of trouble." He slapped them on their backs, nearly knocking them over as he easily reached down and picked up his and Susan's luggage. "Don't worry, I'll call when I need your help. Take those hot women home and try to get some rest." Gene snickered and went to round up his wife and Pogo.

181

"Alright Kids, I'll get us a cab!" Gene kissed Susan and slapped Pogo on the arm, then turn to go inside the terminal when Susan grabbed his arm and pointed toward the gate.

"Looks like we have a ride, sweetheart."

Shirley and Owen Andrews stood waving, each holding one of the twins in their arms. The Scotts and Pogo picked up their luggage and started walking quickly toward their family. With only a few more feet away, Gene and Susan sat down their suitcases and squatted down, then threw out their arms for their children. Samson and Delilah came running to their parents, squealing out, "Mommy and daddy!"

Gene picked up his little girl and twirled her around "That's my baby girl! How's daddy's little pumpkin?" he kissed her rosy cheek as she giggled and hugged him around his neck.

Susan had picked up Samson and was giving him kisses and hugs as she smiled over at her husband, making over their daughter. She reached over and rubbed her hand over Delilah's curls.

"Daddy's girl!" Susan turned back to her son and gave him another kiss "Daddy and mommy love our big strong boy too!"

"Di and Samson wuv you too, Mommy!" the young boy who resembled his father, smiled over at Gene with big blue eyes. "We wuv you too, daddy!"

Gene laughed softly as he reached over to kiss his boy's cheek and mess up his curly hair, causing Samson to laugh out.

"Kids, mommy and daddy love you both! I bet you didn't miss us for one minute!"

"We kept them far too busy to miss you." Shirley laughed as she hugged her daughter, then she looked down at the twins, staring at her with big eyes, trying to make out her words. "I must admit, the little dears did ask about you every night when we laid them down."

"I guess grand mom and granddad can't say prayers with

them as good as their mommy and daddy." Owen helped Gene put all the luggage in the big empty trunk "Welcome home kids! Sounds like you had another winning team, Scott!"

"I sure did, Owen, but it's good to be back home." Gene helped fasten the children in their seats as he looked around at Shirley. "These little young'uns are growing like weeds, Shirley. What did you feed them, growing sprouts?"

"Get in that car, Gene Scott! Let's get you home!" Shirley Andrews laughed "The church awaits!"

Jobi ran from his cabin when he saw Pogo returning to the church camp with the supplies needed for the youth groups retreat. Susan's brother dashed out to meet him with orders from their brave camp leader, Gene Scott. Pogo climbed out of the station wagon and looked around at the empty camp.

"Jobi, where is everybody? I thought Scott was going to wait here until I return with these supplies!" Pogo climbed out and started unloading several big boxes.

"They are waiting for me at the west trail. Scott is taking us to the top this morning, Echo Ridge! He wants you to get lunch ready by twelve noon. I'm supposed to help you with these supplies then hurry back for the climb." Jobi started to reach for a box when Pogo held out a letter with the word, URGENT, written boldly on the envelope.

"Jobi, forget the boxes, buddy! I need you to take this letter straight to Scott! It looks pretty important!"

The young boy noticed the postmark was from Africa. His attention grew to the handwriting, his eye grew wide, filled with questions.

"Hey, this is from granddad! I'll take it right now!" he took the letter nervously as Pogo held his arm.

"Good! Take it, and kid, send Ben and Johnny back to help me unload these things and carry them to the mess hall." Pogo kept unloading the station wagon as he watched Jobi race up the deep slope.

Gene Scott checked his watch, then stepped inside the circle of noisy teens. He held his hands up and whistled loudly to get their attention.

"Listen up kids, as soon as Jobi gets back, we are heading up the path to Echo Ridge! Has everyone got water?"

All the excited teen held up their canteens, hanging around their necks. Three of the young girls stood in their own small circle, their heads close together as they whispered about the handsome preacher.

"Reverend Scott looks so cool and dreamy in those khaki shorts, blue shirt and hiking boots!"

"Susan is dressed just like him and she always looks beautiful." Annie Fletcher added shyly "I think they make a perfect couple."

"Susan is alright, I guess, but really Annie, I think 'Gene' and I would look totally cool together!" Bessie Turner smiled dreamingly.

Susan had stopped to tie her boot tighter when she noticed the three teenage girls staring at her husband. She could tell by their whispering and drooling, they were discussing him. She walked casually behind the girls, not much younger than herself, and patted them lightly on the back, startling each girl.

"Girls, I hope you are ready for this strenuous hike up to Echo Ridge! I think you need to save your breath for the high altitude!" Susan's eyebrow arched as her voice grew stern "A word of good advice, ladies! Stop dreaming about my man! Do you understand?"

The girls swallowed as they looked at one another, worried that Susan had heard their words. Their hearts fell when the handsome preacher looked their way and called out to his wife.

"Is there anything wrong over there, sweetheart?"

"No, not now, darling! I think these girls know what is expected of them!" Susan looked them in the eye "And know what to stay away from!"

Jobi came running up to Gene, filled with anxious excitement.

"Reverend Scott!" Jobi had to catch his breath as he bent over and put his hands on his knees. He had made the twenty-minute walk up to the west trail in less than seven minutes. "I...I..."

"Hey buddy, slow down and catch your breath! Has something happened to Pogo?"

"Pogo? Oh, no sir, but..." Jobi looked around the group of listening teens until he spotted the two he was looking for "Ben, you and Johnny need to go and help Pogo unload the car!" The young man gasp for breath as Gene helped him stand straight.

"So, what is so important, young man, to make you race up that steep path at neck breaking speed?"

"Scott, a letter came for you! It's from granddad and it looks real important!" Jobi handed the letter to Gene, his eyes wide with concern.

"Granddad?" Susan raced over and look down at the bold letters in her granddad's handwriting. "It is from him!"

Gene opened the letter quickly and read Doctor Roger's words out loud for the Andrews siblings to hear.

"Reverend Scott, you know I would not ask you for your help unless I thought it necessary. I have run into some trouble here on my land and even though I tried to handle the situation on my own, it has gotten out of hand. I know Susan and Jobi will want to help you, so you might as well bring my grandchildren along with you. This will save you from worrying about them traveling along behind you. Your Susan would just follow you anyway and Jobi would insist she bring him to help." Gene stopped reading long enough to smile down at his wife. She made a face at him and mumbled.

"Just keep reading, reverend! Does he mention what is wrong?"

"Scott, it might get dangerous. My instincts tell me it will, so bring some protection with you. I have several weapons myself, hunting rifles, pistols, and many different bush and hunting knives. Please be careful! Tell Shirley and Owen I want the three of you to visit. Make excuses why you cannot bring those little twins along. I would love to see them someday, not just now, if you catch my meaning.

Enclosed are three one- way airline tickets to the Taboo Airport. You might recall it is nothing fancy and quite small but it has a nice long run way. My way of thanking you for your much -needed help, I will be sending you back home on the ocean liner that brought you here two years ago. The same ship line you love birds met on. I hope it will bring back happy memories. After you port in North Carolina, you will take a straight flight to L A, then back home to TarSa.

Scott, I urge you to hurry and not delay! God speed, my friend!" Dr. William T. Rogers

"Oh, Gene, granddad is in some kind of big trouble! We must go at once!" Susan pulled at his arm as she looked around at all the sad faces reflecting off the teenagers.

"Alright! This is the plan! I will go call John and have him send replacements for us here at Camp Lookout while you go home and pack our things then call your parents!" Gene quickly checked the airline tickets "Our flight to L A leaves early in the morning, so there's no time to lose." He pulled Jobi over "Son, you go tell Pogo what has happened and have him drive you straight to your house to pack. Tell him I will get someone to replace him as camp cook because I will need him to watch the home front." Gene thought a second, knowing how his young friend gets his feelings hurt when it comes to his cooking "Tell him, I said it won't be easy to replace him but they will have to take second best."

Even with the bad situation over his grandfather, Jobi chuckled, knowing Scott didn't wish to hurt his pal's feelings. Scott turned him around to face the path down and gave him a little push as his attention fell on Susan.

"Alright, what are you kids waiting for? Move those butts!" Gene clapped his hands to get the teens attention as he smiled at the Andrews siblings running down the hill. "We've been called away on a family fun get-away!" He didn't want anyone to know the real reason for their sudden exit. "Replacements are coming and stop looking so darn sad! You can have fun together without us! Now follow me down to the camp until John sends your new leaders." He noticed their long faces "And cheer up!"

Chapter Thirty

Gene Scott pulled his station wagon to a stop in front of the Andrews' large mansion. He glanced over at Susan who sat staring from her window in deep thought.

"Well, Mrs. Scott, are you going to fill me in on what you and Jobi came up with to tell your parents?"

"Just follow our lead Reverend Scott and fill in any gaps we might miss." She reached over and kissed his worried face "Darling, just relax! Don't you know by now the Andrews siblings can always fool their parents!" she hopped out and started taking her daughter out of her car seat. She glanced up at Gene, still sating behind the wheel, staring back at her. "Daddy, can you get your son ready and stop staring at me!"

Gene shook his head as he climbed from the car and started taking Samson out of his seat.

"Yeh, kid" he spoke to his son as he lifted him up into his arms "Your sweet mommy has been giving me orders ever since our honeymoon. When it comes to women, my boy, you do not stand a chance." The little face, that looked much like his father, blinked at his words. Gene studied his face and shook his head "Shit son, you look just like your old man!"

"Gene Scott, behave yourself this instant!" Susan laughed "But you are correct darling, Samson looks just like his wonderful, handsome daddy!"

"Hey Susan, I got the kid's stuff unloaded and carried up to the front door!" Pogo reached over and pinched Delilah's rosy cheek and made her giggle "Are you sure you guys don't need my help on this adventure?"

"No pal! I need you to stay here and look after everything at home. That grass needs constant attention!" Scott looped his arm over Pogo's shoulder "Who knows pal, you might find time to ask one of those sweet young ladies from church out for a date."

Gene started up the sidewalk, Pogo right behind him. He was glad Gene brought up dating."

"Speaking of dates, it's funny you should say that Scott. I just happen to have a date for Saturday night."

"A date?" Gene stopped and smiled down at his young friend "I knew you had your eye on one of those cute girls! Which one did you choose, slugger?"

"Oh look, there's Shirley and Owen! Hi guys! It's good to see you again, Mr. and Mrs. Andrews. Are you ready to baby sit again?"

"We certainly are, Pogo. The children are a delight!" Shirley reached for her granddaughter "There is my sweet girl. You look more like your mama every day, Di."

"Shirley's right, these children sure are the spitting image of the both of you!" Owen took Samson from Gene "My little man." Susan's father smiled over at her as he kissed her "So, you are off to see William. Let me see…" Owen thought for a minute "it has been two years since you and Jobi visited your granddad in Africa."

"That's right, two years and they have flown by, dad." Susan smiled at her brother, who was bringing his big suitcase down the steps "Hi Jobi! I hope you brought some long sleeve shirts and pants along for the Safari."

"You bet I did, sis! I packed my new camera with the zoom lens to take lots of big game shots!" Jobi smile up at Scott "I still can't believe it Reverend Scott, my very first Safari! Wow!"

"It was so thoughtful of granddad to think of inviting the three of us, to tag along with him on his very first Safari tour! If anyone knows the African plane, it's granddad!" Susan hugged her father while Gene stared at the brother and sister with astonishment "Oh dad, doesn't it sound great! Granddad calls it: Roger's Safari Adventures and he offered us the last three spaces!"

"Yeh! Granddad knows how we are always asking about

different wild animals as well as strange plants and natives!" Jobi beamed "That grandad is really cool and he knows we love hanging around with him! He even said I would be sharing a tent with him, knowing Reverend Scott and Susan would need a tent of their own."

Gene Scott cleared his throat as he frowned at the brother and sister.

"So, that is the reason we ask you to watch our pumpkins while we are away, having such a grand time with William!" Gene glanced over at his silent young friend, who stood staring at the siblings with his mouth open. The preacher reached over and punched him. "With my pal Pogo watching the home front and my favorite in-laws taking care of our young'uns, everything will work out great!" Gene slapped Owen's back lightly, causing him to give a little cough. Susan's father smiled sheepishly, aware of Scott's great strength and his putting off going to the gym himself "That is…if it's alright with you? It hasn't been that long since my last mission and now we are putting them back on you?"

Susan and Jobi glared up at Scott with anxious expressions, hoping their parents would not have, second thoughts and decline their request. There worries were quickly vanished when Mildred came running from the house, drying her hands on a dish towel.

"Where are those babies? Where are my little angels?" As Mildred got down on her knees and held out her arms to the twins, Susan and Jobi let out a breath of relief. "There you are! Come here and give old Mildred a hug!"

Samson and Delilah scrambled out of their grandparent's arms and raced to Mildred, calling "Milly! Milly!" as they giggled after every kiss from the jolly woman. Mildred looked up at the Scotts, her eyes filled with love and joy.

"Now, don't you worry none about your babies, do you hear? Stay as long as you like, Reverend Scott, Susan, dear! These little bundles bring a lot of life and joy in this big house!

Yes, yes, indeed!" Mildred stood up and tenderly took each child's hand, real love shining from her eyes "It brings back fond memories of helping raise Miss Susan and Master Jobi when they were small. It doesn't seem like that long ago, no sir-ri."

"It wasn't that long- ago Mildred!" Gene took his wife's hand "There are times when my sweet Susan still acts like a little girl."

"And you really enjoy me on those nights, darling." Susan smile slyly, knowing she had turned the table on her husband.

Shirley Andrews turned a bright shade of pink from her daughter's remark. Gene forced a smile at Susan's mother and squeezed his wife's hand tightly as a warning for her to behave. Even though the pain in her hand was bad, Susan tried to act naturally as she laughed.

"Oh mom, you know I'm kidding." Susan looked over at her brother for help.

"Mom, these two tease one another all the time. Sis always gets the last one on Scott, every time!" Jobi quickly moved behind Pogo when Gene took a step toward him, frowning.

Owen laughed and hugged his daughter "Shirley, give these kids a break, dear. You should know by now, they love picking with one another." He rubbed his hand over Jobi's head and smiled up at the handsome preacher "Just have a good time, all three of you. After that trying case you just solved, you deserve to have a little fun." Owen walked his son-in-law to the car and spoke softly "Reverend Scott, I know you have your hands full with my two, but I trust you watching them more than anyone I know."

"Thank you for that Owen. Your Jobi can be a handful sometime, but he is a very special young man." Scott patted Susan's brother's arm, then smiled down at his wife "As for Susan, I just thank God you and Shirley had such a beautiful, exciting, outgoing, and loving daughter and you did not fight our love when Susan was so much younger than me." Gene put his arm around Susan and pulled her close to him "I love this woman more than I have loved anyone or anything, so, you do not have to worry about their welfare or safety ever, as long as I live. I will guard them with my life and that is a promise easily kept."

"I just thank God you came into one another's life!" Shirley stood on her tiptoes to hug the handsome preacher "Just have a great time with father and an even better time on that ship when you return. The same ocean liner you and Susan met on and instantly fell in love. How romantic!"

"We intend to make the most of it, mom." Susan smiled up at her husband "Relive some of those beautiful memories."

"And make a lot of new ones, little darling!" Gene hit Susan on her butt "Now, let's start making memories, Mrs. Scott!" Gene kissed his children one last time "You two little Scotts, be good and listen to your grand mom and grand dad!" he winked at Mildred, who was holding on to Samson and Delilah "And let your Milly spoil you!"

"Not too much, Mildred." Susan bent down to hold her twins tight and shower them with motherly kisses "Remember, my darlings, mommy and daddy loves you very much!"

"We wuv you too, Mommy and Daddy!" the twins called out in unison. Everyone laughed and waved as the station wagon drove toward the TarSa Airport.

Scott pulled his car as close to the gate as possible and handed the keys to his young friend.

"Alright Pogo, just be careful."

"What? On my date?" Pogo helped Scott with their luggage, keeping his eyes on the bags.

"No buddy, I meant be careful driving, mowing, cleaning and cooking." Gene narrowed his eyes at Pogo "You still have not told me who you are dating Saturday night, pal."

"Dating? Pogo?" Susan hugged him, smiling "Pogo, that's

great! You can drive the Corvette if you like."

"Thanks a lot, Susan! That's real heavy!" Pogo tried to avoid Scott's stare when he noticed their blue- eyed pilot waving "Look guys, there's Mike! Looks like he is ready for you. He is waving beside his plane."

"Are you going to tell me who this girl is or not, Pogo? I'm not budging till you do!"

"Listen Scott, you had your secret girl, remember?" Pogo laughed sheepishly as he slapped his big friend on the back. An instant pain shot through his hand "Damn Scott! I keep forgetting, you are solid steel" he shook his hand.

"You listen pal, I'll help you remember just how strong I am if you do not spit out this girl's name, right now!" Scott bent down and stared his young friend in the eyes as his voice grew louder and more demanding "I am waiting, Pogo!"

"Gene, sweetheart, just let Pogo have his little secret for a while." Susan winked at her blushing friend and picked up a small suitcase "Now, grab our luggage darling. Mike is waiting and Jobi is already climbed on, not to mention we have a plane to catch in L A."

"Shit! Pogo, I have enough to worry about with whatever the shit is going on with Susan's granddad and keeping my eye out for those two kids, without worrying about you and who you are going out with! Why the big secret? Why won't you tell your old pal?"

"Scott, stop worrying about me. There is really nothing to worry about." Pogo forced a laugh "I will tell you when you get back, but for now, let me have my secret. You can trust me to be smart, Scott. The truth is, every time I tell you about a girl I'm interested in, you seem to jinx it or something. Girls always fall for you, man, but I have to work at it. Just go, before you miss your plane! Go and have fun on that ship after you help Doctor Rogers. Just, don't worry about your pal, Pogo." He reached up and touched his serious friend's shoulder "I will share this much. She is a good Methodist

Christian, Scott, I promise!"

"Oh, alright, Pogo." Scott waved back at Mike as he picked up his and Susan's luggage, then turned his attention back on his young friend, who appeared more relaxed. "I'm dropping it for now, buddy, only because the plane is ready to leave and I have a deadline. To quote Lincoln, 'One war at a time!" shaking his head, Gene Scott went to join Susan on the plane.

Jackie waved from the back of Michael's airplane when Gene climbed aboard. "Hi Scott, good of you to join us! Grab the seat next to Mike. Susan and I need to catch up."

"You bet, beautiful! I'm sorry if I held you up, issues with the kid!" After he and Michael had stored the luggage safely away, the two handsome men buckled their belts for take-off. "It's back to the dangers of Africa for us, Mike!"

"I don't envy you folks one bit." Michael flew his plane up with ease "But seriously Scott, if you need our help once you get there, please give us a shout! James and I will be standing by." He looked up at the back seat and smiled at Jackie, who blew him a kiss. "Our women will be more than happy to assist us and gladly do their part. We can be in Africa as fast as I can fly this bird!"

"Thank you, Mike, I will certainly keep your offer in mind. There is not another group I'd choose but the four of you." Scott took in the vast sky and watched the land below grow smaller as the plane went higher. "I don't know what we will run into once we reach Roger's ranch."

"A big mystery, ah?' Michael looked around him, feeling free high in the air "I never get tired of this view, Scott. It's like flying around in heaven!"

"It is quite spectacular up here." Scott felt a pat on his back and turned to see Jackie smiling down.

"Reverend Scott, Susan tells me that her first ship romance happened two years ago on the very ship you will be sailing on when you return to the mainland. Gene, I am so excited for you and Susan! I hope you have the time of your life, darling."

"We certainly plan to, Jackie." Scott turned to see Jobi watching the clouds float by "That is, if we can keep that one busy."

"Now that Jobi is fourteen, I would think staying in his own cabin would be…what do kids say?"

"Heavy Jackie! We say, heavy!" Michael reached back and patted her shapely leg. "Jackie came along because she didn't want me to fly home by myself. This girl is crazy about her man."

Jackie hit Michael playfully and laughed "Somebody has got to watch over you, darling. So, it might as well be me. After all, we share the same bed."

"By the way, I never ask you." Gene looked at the handsome couple "When did you two, start sharing that bed?" Jackie's eyes widen as the preacher continued "How long have you kids been married."

Susan sat up straight when she heard Gene's question. She called up to the front, to help her nervous friends.

"Jackie, can you come back here and give me a hand?" Susan knew how her husband felt about couples shacking up, as he called it. If their secret came out, Gene would explode. Jackie took a relief breath as she answered.

"Coming Susan!" she patted Michael's arm "Mike, keep your mind on flying darling. It looks like a 'STORM' is about to come up out there!"

"Got 'sh, sweetheart! I see what you mean." Catching his lovers meaning, Mike took the controls firmly and smiled over to Gene. "Can we discuss our married bliss later, Scott? These clouds look threating."

"What? Those fluffy little clouds?" Scott scanned the sky, clear with a few white clouds "It looks perfectly fine to me."

"Scott, after you have flown as much as me and Jackie, you noticed the little things that can be a warning. It pays to stay alert, just in case." Michael's eyes danced with mischief

"Believe me, my friend, after you have been married for as long as we have, you start to noticed the same thing."

Gene Scott laid his head back on the head rack and closed his eyes as he mumbled to himself.

"You are absolutely right, honest Abe, One damn war at a time!"

Chapter Thirty-One

Pogo drove away from the airport smiling to himself as he traveled along down the busy highway.

"I got Scott worrying about my mystery date! He would really be upset if he knew who she was. Miss redhead herself, Gloria Ann Weber!" stopping the car in front of the white farmhouse. Pogo glanced over at the yellow Corvette, parked in the outside garage. His heart was racing with excitement when he climbed out of the family station wagon and ran up to unlock the door.

"I will be driving in style thanks to Susan and I know just what I'm going to wear! I think I was pretty smart to save the black silk pants and sport coat I wore in Texas!" he stopped and looked at his refection in the hall mirror, a regular looking teenager, in jeans and a t-shirt. He made a face at himself.

"I'm plain now, yes, but when I put on that hot outfit, not to brag on myself, but I looked pretty damn sexy in it! I even got a few winks from some of Joe's hookers!" he danced up the steps "Miss Weber is in for a real treat!"

Saturday rolled around and the evening for Pogo's big date with the bishop's daughter. Looking in the floor-length mirror that set in the master bedroom, Pogo's smile showed his approval. Decked in the black silk shirt and sport coat, the young man looked more mature and quite handsome. After checking his wallet to make sure he had the cash that had been put away from working for Scott, doing everything around the farm, like, cooking, mowing, cleaning, gardening, and helping Susan with the twins, he found he had plenty, plus the credit card Scott had gave him, to use for home expenses.

"Maybe Scott wouldn't mind me having one super night on him." Pogo walked into Gene and Susan's bathroom to find

Scott's aftershave. "Scott always keeps a spare bottle of Polo Aftershave stored in his bathroom closet." Opening the closet door, he spotted the signature green box "I don't think my old pal will mind if I use some of his Polo. I may make a few points with Gloria if I smell like the man she adores!" Pogo set the opened green bottle back on the shelf, knowing Gene would wonder how it got open. "I will tell Scott I borrowed some for my date because I wanted to smell as good as him, since he always draws the ladies!"

As he shut the door to the master bedroom, his attention went to his gold watch, a Christmas present from Gene and Susan. He started to feel a little guilty that he hadn't told his best friend about his date with the redhead. As he reached the front hall, his eyes where drawn to a portrait of Gene and Susan. It was as if the handsome preacher was looking right into the young man's eyes, making him feel nervous.

"Look Scott, if I would have told you my date was Gloria Ann Weber, you would have put a stop to it! It's just this one time, man! You know her, she will find me cheap, poor, and boring. But, for now, I just want to go out on a limb and have a little fun! I say, what you don't know, won't hurt...me!" Pogo jumped when the grandfather clock stroke seven. He glanced nervously at his watch and swallowed. If he wanted to be on time, he had to leave immediately. Starting out on the wrong foot with Miss Weber was not wise.

Pogo raced out and climbed in Susan's car. It fit his mood perfect and after checking the gas gage, he saw the hand was on full.

"That's our sweet Susan, always on top of everything! Why, if she didn't belong to my best friend..." Pogo glanced in the mirror and he could imagine Gene's frowning face "better stop while I am ahead! I got a hot woman waiting!" he laughed as he drove out of the driveway and headed toward the rich side of town.

As Pogo drove through the massive gates, he suddenly felt

butterflies invade his stomach and started having second thoughts when the Weber mansion came into view.

"What are you thinking, Pogo Goings? Shit, you are just some dumb poor kid, this gal is disgustingly rich!" he stopped the Corvette and stared up at the house, towering above him. "They will just laugh at me!" Pogo sat straight up when the front door opened and Gloria Ann walked out, dressed in a low cut, red dress, a light mink jacket over her soft slim shoulder. Pogo's hand shook as he opened the door and got out. He whispered softly to himself "Here goes kid, be brave!"

"Pogo, darling!" Gloria Ann Weber smiled brightly and waved at the handsome young man. Her green eyes traveled the full length of his body. "Pogo, you look terrific, so…handsome and mature." She placed her soft hand on his arm "This night is going to be better than I had imagined!"

"You look exceptionally beautiful yourself, Gloria." Pogo stood tall as he stretched his 6'2" frame "Do you mind riding in my car or had you rather take yours?" He remembered her dislikes of Gene's cars.

"Pogo darling, you are such a dear." She glanced down at the yellow Corvette and smiled brightly "Your car will be perfect sweetheart. I would truly be proud to be seen with you in anything."

Feeling more relaxed Pogo smiled, as he opened the door for her and watched as she slid in, showing her shapely legs. Her soft voice drew his eyes away from her legs to her alluring green eyes.

"Like what you see Pogo?" she teased "Play your cards right and they could be yours."

Blushing a bright red Pogo closed her door and walked around to get in next to her. He glanced one more time at the Weber mansion and was glad he didn't have to face her parents. Leaving the big estate behind, he managed to sound normal when he reached the end of the long private driveway.

"Where to?" Pogo kept his attention on the road in front of

him "You said you knew a perfect place for dining and dancing."

"Yes darling! Just turn left and stay on Country Forest Drive until you come to Beverly Avenue." Gloria checked her reflection in the mirror "The Red Fox Tavern is the perfect place for a romantic night out." Her hand fell on Pogo's leg. "There is no one waiting up for you at home, is there darling? What I'm asking is, do you have a curfew?"

"No Gloria, I do not have a curfew! There is no one at home right now. Gene and Susan are visiting Susan's grandfather in Africa." The nervous young man swallowed, wondering why this beautiful woman wanted to know these things about him and what could possibly be on her mind. At last Pogo turned to look into her serious green eyes "Besides Gloria, I'm old enough to stay out as long as I like."

"But, I bet you didn't tell Gene I was your date, did you?" Gloria spoke softly, her eyes sincere and Pogo saw something different in her eyes, something he had never seen from her before. Her flirty teasing tone was gone and was replaced with sincere emotion.

"You know Scott, he…well…he would just think you were using me Gloria, to get to him." Pogo could not pull himself away from her sad face "He would think that Gloria, if I told him."

"Then Gene Scott would be wrong!" Gloria reached over and gently touched Pogo's tan face "I am really into you Pogo. I think we could become something special." She pulled her hand away and turned to stare from the window. "I can't explain it! Ever since we spoke that day before you took off for Texas, I have thought of nothing but you, you and me."

Pogo pulled the car over by the curb and stopped. He turned around in the seat and looked at her.

"Gloria, are you just saying these things because you want to make Scott jealous?"

"Pogo, the honest truth is, I have not thought about Gene

one time since that day! Why should I? Gene is married, married and happy!" tears began to run down her cheeks "He doesn't want me, Gene has never wanted me! And that was long before he met Susan! Then Susan came into his life and stole his heart and my chance was gone forever, not that there ever was one in the first place!"

"What are you trying to say to me Gloria?" Pogo searched her green eyes for an answer and found them laced with real tears.

"I can't explain it Pogo! This thing I'm feeling, is new to me! I don't know when it happened or why, but…" she looked deep into his eyes "I fell in love with you, Pogo."

"Love? Gloria?" Pogo reached for her soft hand "I have nothing to offer you. I had no one until Scott and his first wife took me in and made me a part of their family. Scott is all I have!" he didn't know how to feel about this beautiful wealthy woman declaring her love to him, a nobody. He hadn't expected this. "Gloria, you have everything you want. You are rich and beautiful, the bishop's only daughter. Your parents could never except me to be part of your life! Scott is my best friend in the entire world! I could never hurt him!"

"Is that the real reason you didn't tell him about our date Pogo?" Gloria looked hurt from deep within. "You thought you would have one secret date with rich Gloria Ann Weber, then you could brag to all your friends about dating an older rich lady!" Gloria could not control the flood of tears that fell from her eyes as her voice began to break up "Yes, I'm rich! Yes, my father buys me everything I want! But God help me Pogo Goings, I would give it all up for you! I thought I love Gene Scott. But I would have never given up my lifestyle for him or any other man I dated, until…you came into my heart!"

Gloria opened the car door and jumped out "Go ahead, go back where it's safe! You don't really owe me a thing! Maybe we were meant for each other, but I guess we will never know! But…the thing is, I know! I love you Pogo!" Needing to get away from his questioning eyes, the eyes of the young man she had just declared her love to, she slipped off her heels and started running down the sidewalk, lit only by the streetlights, tears blinding her way.

Pogo jumped out of the Corvette and took off after her, his mind whirling in a million directions. He caught her on the edge of the park and pulled her around into his arms, holding her close.

"Gloria, sweetheart!" Pogo's lips melted over hers as she held him tight around the neck, caught up in the passion. His voice came soft in her ear "I can't explain what I'm feeling right now Gloria. I just know when you spoke those words to me and told me you loved me, I felt something new, exciting and beautiful happening inside me, all at once!"

"Maybe what you feel is love Pogo." Gloria looked deeply into his warm brown eyes and saw her reflection from the gas-lit park lantern. To his amazement, he could also see his reflection in her serious green eyes, glistening with love "Do you think it can be love? Do you love me Pogo?"

His lips were once again drawn to her luscious lips where they burned down over them. His breathing came heavy as he whispered

"Gloria, I do love you! I can't explain it no more than you, how it happened, but I know how I feel and I know without a doubt, I love you Gloria Ann Weber!"

Pogo held on to her tightly, his heart racing with new love. Suddenly the reality of the situation hit him and he squeezed his eyes closed as he thought to himself

"Shit, Scott is going to kill me!"

AUTHOR'S NOTES

The Scotts head off on another exciting mission, filled with danger, kidnapping, and diamond thieves!

Pogo and Gloria find themselves in the same secret situation that Gene and Susan were in. A beautiful new love that no one would except, especially Pogo's best friend, Reverend Gene Scott! The great change in the bishop's daughter was unbelievable to her parents and those who knew her. They only knew this new secret man in her life had made her heart turn to pure unselfish love.

Gene and Susan's love continues to grow stronger everyday as is the preacher's vow to the girl he gave his heart to. The vow to love her and to spend the rest of his life with her, declaring "I will always be KEEPING WATCH OVER YOU, my darling Susan, for All My Tomorrows!"

BOOK 4 *KEEPING WATCH OVER YOU*

And Coming Soon,

BOOK 5: *LOVE NEVER ENDS*

By JOAN BYRD